T0267929

JOHN SCHU

With a foreword by Kate DiCamillo

THORNDIKE PRESS
A part of Gale, a Cengage Company

Thorndike Press, a part of Gale, a Cengage Company.

**LIBRARY OF CONGRESS CIP DATA ON FILE.
CATALOGUING IN PUBLICATION FOR THIS BOOK
IS AVAILABLE FROM THE LIBRARY OF CONGRESS.**

ISBN-13: 978-1-4205-1715-6 (hardcover alk. paper)

Published in 2024 by arrangement with Candlewick Press.

Print Number: 1   Print Year: 2025
Printed in Mexico

For Grandma Ruth,
who always reminded me
to slow down.

For Molly O'Neill,
who said,
"There's a story here!
Keep writing!"

For every teenager
who imagines performing
on Broadway one day.

For thirteen-year-old me,
who needed a book
like this one.

A Foreword

What if someone was brave enough to tell you the truth?

What if someone dared to reveal their heart to you?

The book that you hold in your hands tells a painful truth.

It reveals a beautiful, broken heart.

Jake's heart.

Jake is thirteen years old, and he has an eating disorder.

You and Jake are about to go on a harrowing journey together; by the time you finish this book, you will be friends.

Reading Jake's story will change you.

You might find that you want to reveal your heart, tell someone your truth.

Telling your story can save your life.

It may save someone else's life, too.

Jake knows this.

John Schu knows this.

That is why he wrote this book.

For you.

— Kate DiCamillo

Jake Stacey

Grade: 8

Year: 1996

Favorite Subject: Language Arts

Favorite Book: *The Giver* by Lois Lowry

Favorite Movie: *Home Alone*

Favorite Sport: Rollerblading

Favorite Food:

A Goal: To see a musical on Broadway with Grandma

Writing My Name

I write

Jake

in
cursive

over

and

over

and

over.

It's
calming.

Filling
page after page
in my notebooks
with signatures.

Using
different
colors.

Purple.

Green.

Blue.

It's
soothing.

Trying out
different
styles.

Fancy.

Plain.

Bold.

Experimenting with

markers,   highlighters,   pastels.

Why is it
calming?

Why is it
soothing?

Maybe
because
I'm hoping
by writing
my name
over
and
over,
I'll
figure
out

who
I
am.

Jake

Jake

Jake

Jake

Jake

Jake

Jake

Nobody?

....

My stomach
G-R-O-W-L-S.

The Voice
tells it
to

S

   T

      O

        P.

I toss the markers
inside the top drawer
of my desk.

I tear out the page
and rip it up
into little bits,
dropping each

piece into the
garbage can.

I look at a photo of
Emily Dickinson
taped to my desk.

I know
her poem
"I'm Nobody! Who are you?"
by heart.

So I run in place,
burning as many calories as I can,
repeating
the opening lines

I'm Nobody! Who are you?
Are you — Nobody — too?

as
FAST
as
I
can.

I'm Nobody! Who are you?
Are you — Nobody — too?

I'm Nobody! Who are you?
Are you — Nobody — too?

The Voice says,

YOU — ARE — REPULSIVE!

Am I Nobody,
Too?

....

When I can't run anymore
I sit down again at my
big brown desk.

Mom
knocks, knocks, knocks
on my bedroom door.

I ignore her.

KNOCK. KNOCK. KNOCK.

I don't have
enough energy
to tell her to
GO AWAY —
to leave me alone.

I wish everyone
would leave me alone —
forever.

KNOCK. KNOCK. KNOCK.

Worry enters the room.

She brings it
wherever she goes.

You can feel it.

Smell it.

Mom puts a plate of
pretzels and pepperoni
on my desk next to me.

My stomach
G-R-O-W-L-S
        again.

The Voice says,

DON'T EAT THAT GARBAGE!

YOU ALREADY ATE AN APPLE TODAY!

YOU DIDN'T EXERCISE ENOUGH!

She says,

Why haven't you started your homework?

This isn't like you.

What's going on?

I want to say,

This isn't like you.

You don't usually care.

I glare at
math
problems,

wishing
X and Y
would
run away.

I imagine
feeding the
garbage
disposal
pretzels,
pepperoni, and
these
wretched
worksheets,
watching
it
grind
everything
into
tiny
bits.

The Voice

....

The
negative
Voice
inside
my
head
talks
nonstop.

It
has
since
the
middle
of
seventh
grade.

It's
louder

than
the
hunger
in
my
stomach.

I
weigh
myself
10
times
per
day.

Then
15
times
per
day.

Then
20
times
per
day.

The
lower
the
number
on
the
scale
goes,
the
bigger
I
feel.

The
bigger
I
feel,
the
less
I
eat.

The
less
I

eat,
the
less
I
feel.

I
make
my
body
smaller
and
smaller
and
smaller.

I
punish
myself
day
after
day.

Why?

For
taking
up
too
much
space.

For
being
me.

For
breathing.

Clothes

···············

I own
two pairs of
overalls:
one denim,
one corduroy.

I wear
a pair
every day
to school.

Sometimes
I wear a big sweatshirt
over the overalls.

Most
people
think
it's
strange.

But
waistbands,
seams,
fabrics
make me feel
itchy,
gross.

Aware of
every inch of my body,
every movement.

Aware of
how the denim
touches my
collarbone.

Aware of
how the corduroy
rubs against my
thigh.

Aware of
how my body

feels at every
moment:
itchy,
gross,
growing.

I Hate
Eighth Grade

I'm in Language Arts class.

I think about Emily Dickinson's photo.

I think about her kind eyes.

    Emily, eighth grade's hard.

Hard to concentrate.

Hard to smile.

Hard to eat.

    Emily, eighth grade hurts.

I wish I could go back to fourth grade.

I was happy in Ms. Wozny's class.

Happy when she told knock-knock jokes,
sang silly songs,
recited poems about chicken soup with
  rice.
She read aloud to us every day after
  lunch-recess.

We would gather together on the carpet,
the place where we shared stories.

Stories about fourth graders like us
going on adventures.

Stories about
giants and gold.

Stories that
made everyone laugh.

Stories that
made everyone belong.

Happy when Danielle's desk
was next to mine.

We always talked about how much we
  loved our Star Wars and
Teenage Mutant Ninja Turtles action
  figures.

Emily, will I ever feel happy again
  at school?

Walking Home

....

I walk home from school
lost inside
my mind.

The Voice
helped me skip
lunch today.

The Voice
helped me lie
about why
I didn't turn in my
homework today.

The Voice speaks

LOUDER

and

LOUDER

and

LOUDER

at school.

Skating

As soon as I get home,
I put *Hello, Dolly!*'s
movie musical soundtrack
into a portable
CD player.

It stars Barbra Streisand
as Dolly Levi.

I love her
voice.

I love her
clothes.

I love her big
personality.

She sparkles
like glitter
as Dolly Levi.

I put on headphones.

I hear Barbra's
magical
voice sing out.

I put on Rollerblades.

I skate up and down Kimberly Drive
in our suffocating south suburb of Chicago.

Barbra helps me breathe.

I skate around a small park at the end of
my block.

I skate and skate and skate.

Singing along
with Barbra
at the TOP
of my voice.

Imagining Barbra's beside me
on a big, bright Broadway stage.

Skating,
        singing.
                Singing,
                        skating.

We

    G   *L*   *I*   *D*   *E*

              d

              o

              w

              n

the street.

Skating,

skating,

skating.

Twirling,

twirling,

twirling.

I bend.
        I beam.

                I bounce
                as I burn
                calories.

I pass
a group of
kids from school.
They're
skateboarding
D
O
W
N
the middle of the street.

One of them yells
names
in my direction.
Hateful names
about me.

They laugh.

I repeat in my head,

Don't cry.

        Don't cry.

                Don't cry.

I
stop
the
music.

The Voice says,

YOU NEED TO BURN OFF MORE CALORIES.

I
take
off
as
fast
as
I
can.

I
skate
and
skate,
faster
and
faster,
burning
off
every
last
calorie
left
inside
me.

Ridding
myself of
yesterday's
lunch,
wishing
I didn't
take
up
any
space.

Wishing
I could
skate
far
away.

Grandma

....

Grandma's my
best friend.

OK, my
only friend.

The Voice says,

YOU HAVE ME.

Grandma
Part 2

················

Friday means
Grandma picks me up from school
in her red car.

Friday means
three days away from Mom
and her sadness.

Three days away from Dad,
who's never home anyway.

Three days away from
the names people hurl at me.

Friday means
it's a little easier
to breathe,
a little easier
to be me.

I love Fridays.

Grandma's Favorite Color

Grandma always smells like Big Red gum:
cinnamony spiciness
mixed with a spoonful of comfort.

She loves red things.

Shoes.

Skirts.

Shirts.

Always dressed in red.

Grandma calls red
the color of love
                and warmth
                        and kindness
                                and goodness.

Red,
the color of Grandma.

A
color
I
love.

Chaos Brewing and Beating Inside Even at Grandma's House

....

As Grandma and I watch
our favorite Friday night TV shows
— *Family Matters* and *Full House* —
the Voice
constantly chants and shouts,

YOU DON'T DESERVE

LOVE

AND

WARMTH

AND

KINDNESS

AND

GOODNESS.

YOU DON'T DESERVE

A
N
Y
T
H
I
N
G
!

A Saturday
with Grandma

....

Grandma usually
wakes me up
at 9:00 a.m.

She usually opens
my bedroom door
and sings,

Rise and shine.

It's Saturday.

Are you ready for a day of F-U-N?

It's 11:30 a.m.

She's still sleeping.

The Voice says,

YOU HAVE MORE TIME TO EXERCISE.

A Saturday
with Grandma
Part 2

Grandma asks
if we can skip
our Saturday shopping
and watch *Hello, Dolly!* instead,
a movie we've watched together at least
    fifty times.

I'm relieved.

The Voice
is EXTRA loud
in grocery stores.

My palms sweat,
my heart feels
like it PUMPS blood extra hard
as I read
nutritional label
after
label . . .

Grandma pops popcorn.

She presses play on the VCR.

Grandma: Isn't Barbra Streisand beautiful? I just love this movie. Barbra's voice is like butter.

Grandma laughs.

After a while, she pauses the movie.

Grandma: Why aren't you eating popcorn?

Me: I ate a big bowl of Fruity Pebbles and Life cereal with fruit cocktail on top.

Grandma: Oh, your favorite concoction! I remember how proud you were the first time you made it. I can still see your sweet grin . . .

She is quiet for a minute, remembering. Then . . .

Grandma: But you love our special cheesy popcorn. I added extra cheese powder!

Me: I'm full.

Grandma: You're too thin. I worry. I see it even when you're always wearing those baggy sweaters over your overalls. I don't think you're eating enough. You're a growing boy.

Me: I eat enough. I promise.

Grandma: You need to take care of my boy.

Me: I am. Let's watch the movie. Please press play.

She looks at me and I think she's going to say something more.

Do I want her to?

Then she squeezes my hand and presses
    play and
we sing along with
Dolly Levi,
Cornelius Hackl,
Barnaby Tucker,
Irene Molloy,
and Minnie Fay.

I love Saturdays with Grandma,
even when the Voice makes me lie.

A Nap on Sunday?
Grandma Never Naps

....

Grandma says,

I'm going to lie down for a while.

*Please eat the bowl of spaghetti that's in
    the refrigerator.*

I'll drop you off at the library after my nap.

The Voice says,

YOU CANNOT EAT SPAGHETTI.

I try ignoring the Voice.

I pace around the kitchen,
repeating inside my head:

You can eat spaghetti.

You can eat spaghetti.

You can eat spaghetti.

The Voice says,

YOU CANNOT EAT SPAGHETTI.

I dump the spaghetti down the drain.

A Sunday
at the Library

....

Grandma drops me off
at the public library
for a few hours
before she takes me home.

I always
take in the
NEW BOOK SCENT.

INHALE.

EXHALE.

INHALE.

EXHALE.

There aren't any calories in smelling.

I go downstairs
to the children's section,
browsing the shelves,
looking for my best friends
from elementary school.

I say hello to

📖 *Sarah, Plain and Tall*,

    📖 *Dear Mr. Henshaw*,

        📖 *Shiloh*,

            📖 *Roll of Thunder, Hear My Cry*.

I go back upstairs
to the computer lab.

I find
the most isolated
computer terminal.

My fingers
tremble
over the
keyboard
as I type
anorex . . .

My heart races.

Thump.

Thump.

Thump.

My armpits sweat.

Drip.

Drip.

Drip.

What if someone sees me?

I cannot breathe.

INHALE.

EXHALE.

INHALE.

EXHALE.

What if they find out my secret?

What if they find out

I want

to erase

every

single

thing

about

me?

What if they find out I'm starving myself?

Reflections

....

Near the exit of the library
is the bathroom.

In the bathroom
is a mirror.

In the mirror
is an ugly, grotesque blob
staring back at me,
telling me I'm a
waste of space,
pathetic, worthless.

Is that really me?

I usually avoid mirrors.

Mirrors are
cruel, ruthless.

Do mirrors tell lies?

Sunday in the Park
with Frieden

....

I pace around Pondview Park
next to the library.

The park where Grandma and I
loved to picnic every summer
when I was in elementary school.

The park comforts me
like my favorite blanket
Grandma crocheted for me
when I was two.

It's my special place.

I hear

ducks   quack   quack   quacking,

baseballs   crack   crack   cracking,

babies   cry   cry   crying.

I see
people picnicking.

What does it feel like to eat without worry?

Without a voice constantly
quacking and crying
inside your head?

A voice

pound, pound, pounding

AND

yell, yell, yelling

ALL DAY.

I stare
into the eyes
of a majestic
angel statue.

I named her Frieden
when I was seven.

My secret name for her.

She towers over the park.

She hears everything.

She sees everyone
as she protects
the four cherubs
gathered
beneath her.

Safe.

Loved.

Protected.

There's a flower
in her left hand.

Her right hand
R E A C H E S out,
offering a blessing.

I look into Frieden's
kind eyes.

I beg her
to help me,
to bless me.

I confess today's secrets.

Frieden, I cried this morning eating an
   apple.

Frieden, I lied to Grandma three times
   today.

Frieden, my hair is falling out.

Frieden, soft hair is growing on my
   shoulders.

Frieden, why am I punishing myself?

Frieden, I've lost control.

Frieden, I'm scared.

Frieden, I need help.

Sunday Night

....

Sunday night means
Grandma drives me home
    in her red car.

During our thirty-minute ride,
we always listen to the
Broadway cast recording of our favorite
  musical:
Into the Woods.

It's about fairy-tale characters
who MUST GO

INTO
       THE
             WOODS.

It's about
curses
    and festivals
        and a girl who wears a
        cape as red as blood.

Grandma and I sing about
witches
    and wolves
        and worrying about giants
        roaming around in the sky.

We sing about
    how much the Witch
        loves rutabaga and rampion.

Grandma's quiet as the Baker's Wife
  sings about
how life's made of moments.

She loves this song.

She usually sings along,
but today she doesn't,
so I sing for us both.

Volunteering at the Tinley Terrace

I volunteer
every afternoon
at the Tinley Terrace Nursing Home
for community service hours.

Every eighth grader must complete
   twenty-five hours.

I like helping people.

I like playing Bingo.

I like playing chess and checkers.

I like reading aloud mysteries to blind
   Ms. Burns in room 147.

I like reading comics with Mr. Grant in
   room 155.

I like avoiding people my own age.

I like avoiding home.

I like avoiding food.

Ms. Burns
in Room 147

················

I visit Ms. Burns,
my favorite resident
at the Tinley Terrace,
to read aloud
the latest book
in her favorite
mystery series.

Me: Good afternoon, Ms. Burns!

Ms. Burns: Jake, is that you?

Me: Yes!

Ms. Burns: Thank you for visiting me. I
love when you read to me.

Me: I love reading with you, Ms. Burns.

Ms. Burns: Did you know I was a teacher for thirty-five years?

I read aloud to my students every day.

Stories about brave and bold women.

Stories filled with powerful poetry.

Stories about kind and considerate children like you.

Me: I love when teachers read aloud.

Ms. Burns: Reading aloud is love.

Ms. Burns: May I hold your hand while you read to me?

Me: Yes, Ms. Burns.

Ms. Burns: Jake, are you OK?

Me: Yes.

Ms. Burns: I can feel something is wrong.

I can sense it.

Teachers know these things, Jake.

You've lost a lot of weight.

Are you sick?

Are you eating?

Me: I'm OK.

The Voice hisses,

IGNORE HER!

The Call

....

I'm at my big brown desk
in my bedroom
staring at my homework

Trying not to think about today
when I hear the
kitchen phone ring.

I don't know who is on the other end.
I just know Mom is upset.

She takes the phone into a room
where I cannot hear
everything she's saying.

But I hear her say my name.

I sneak closer.

I hear
the words:
food,
exercise,
restricting . . .

Mom says,

Thank you for calling, Ms. Burns,
and she hangs up the phone.

Why did Ms. Burns call Mom?

Frieden,
Is That You?

....

I wonder,
Frieden,
is
this
your
way
of
helping?

Can't Sleep

....

I toss and turn
thinking about
Mom's phone call.

I turn and toss
thinking about
how for most of my life
Mom's sadness
took up all the space
in our house.

So she ignored me.

Where's Mom?

She's sad,
Dad said.

Why?

She just is.

Why didn't Mom go to work?

She's sad.

Is Mom cooking dinner?

No, she's too sad.

I keep wondering:
Does Mom see I'm sad now?

Tricked

....

The week after Ms. Burns called Mom,
she says I need a check-up.

It seems strange.

An unfamiliar doctor
asks question after question.

Questions about food.

Questions about weight.

Questions about feelings.

I try
lying.

I can't keep the lies straight.

I feel

Trapped!

        Tricked!

                Caught!

Rescued?

....

Did I want
to get
caught?

Result

....

Before I can catch my breath . . .

Before I can process anything . . .

Before the Voice can tell me what to do
  or how to escape . . .

Mom drives me to . . .
                     Whispering Pines.

They trap me inside
              a small intake room

with a
poster of
an eagle
soaring over an
expansive green forest.

I plead with the bird,
asking it to help me

SOAR.

BEGGING

IT

TO

HELP

ME

FLY

OUT

OF

THIS

PLACE.

IMPLORING

IT

TO

SCOOP

ME

UP

AND

DROP

ME

OFF

IN

FRIEDEN'S

PEACEFUL

PARK.

84

They ask me

Question Question Question Question
   After   After   After   After
Question Question Question Question

The Voice says,

LIE!

**DON'T YOU DARE
TELL THE TRUTH!**

But another voice,
one that reminds me of Frieden,
says,

**We need help.
We're going to die.**

Who do I listen to?

Intake

A tall lady enters the room.

She has the
brightest blond hair
I've ever seen.

It shines like
a lighthouse.

Her smile
reminds me of Grandma.

Or is it the Wolf?

The Voice says,

DON'T TRUST HER.

SHE'LL MAKE YOU EAT.

She says,

Hello, Jake! I'm Ruth. I'm a counselor in the eating disorders program.

Me: Hello.

Ruth: How are you feeling?

Me: I don't know.

I'm fine.

Ruth: Jake, we're admitting you for anorexia nervosa. You're dangerously underweight. When you're ready, we'll walk together to the adolescent unit.

Me: What's the adolescent unit?

Ruth: Itsaplacewithotherteenslike youAplacewithprogramsthathelpwith addictionanxietydepressionselfinjury andeatingdisordersAplaceforteenstotalk

Me: Do I have to go?

I'm not like those people.

I don't belong here.

Please, please let me go home.

Ruth: Jake, you need to stay here for a while.

Me: Why are you doing this to me?

Please let me go home.

Ruth: Whenever you're ready, Jake!

Adolescent Unit

....

Ruth leads me down
hallway
after
hallway.

She's so tall.

Tall like the Giant
in *Into the Woods*.

Every hallway looks the same.

A sea of blue walls
and brown numbered doors.

Blue walls.

> Brown doors.

Blue walls.

Brown doors.

It feels like I'm
trapped inside a maze.

It feels as though
I'm hovering above us,
looking down at someone else's life.

She rings a doorbell.

A buzzer sounds.

We walk down another

L   O   N   G

hallway.

Adolescent Unit
Part 2

....

Ruth: This is Nurse Bruce.

Nurse Bruce: Hi, Jake!

The Voice says,

DON'T TRUST HIM.

Me:

Ruth: You're going to go with Nurse Bruce for a few minutes. He's going to ask you some questions and complete your intake. Then I'll take you to your room.

Me: Please let me go home.

I don't belong here.

This is all a big mistake.

Nurse Bruce: We can go whenever you're ready, Jake.

I cannot stop —

I cannot contain —

I cannot hold back
the dam inside me.

I sob and sob and sob and sob and sob
and sob and sob and sob and sob and sob
and sob and sob and sob and sob and sob
and sob and sob and sob and sob and sob
and sob and sob and sob and sob and sob
and sob and sob and sob and sob and sob
and sob and sob and sob and sob and sob
and sob and sob and sob and sob and sob
and sob and sob and sob and sob and sob
and sob and sob and sob and sob and sob
and sob and sob and sob and sob and sob
and sob and sob and sob and sob and sob
and sob and sob and sob and sob and sob
and sob and sob and sob and sob and sob

Nurse Bruce: Are you ready?

Me: OK.

I feel
far
from
OK.

Adolescent Unit
Part 3

....

Nurse Bruce
opens a lonely-looking door.

He tells me to
take off
my shoes,
to remove
both shoelaces.

He asks me to
hand over
my brown belt
as he searches
inside my pockets.

Take off your shirt.

Take off your pants.

Turn around.

He inspects
every
inch
of
my
body.

I feel
exposed.

I feel
confused.

Me: Why are you doing this?

Nurse Bruce: I'm looking for
contraband. I'm looking for anything you
could use to hurt yourself. I'm looking
for bruises and marks on your body.

Me: I wouldn't hurt myself.

Bruce sits next to me.

He smells like coffee . . . and cologne.

There's a small tattoo of a
hummingbird
on his right arm.

Bruce's beard is brown like Dad's.

The Voice says,

DON'T TRUST HIM.

The Voice says,

HE'LL MAKE YOU EAT.

Nurse Bruce says,

Jake, have you looked in a mirror lately?

Room 165

Counselor Ruth
towers over me
as she leads me

D

O

W

N

more

L   O   N   G

hallways.

We stop in front of
room 165.

Ruth says,
This is your room. This is where you'll stay
   for a while.

There's
a bed,
a dresser,
a desk,
a chair,
a closet,
a shut door,
a feeling of dread.

Ruth: Your mom will drop off your
clothes tomorrow morning. There
are pajamas inside the dresser. Extra
blankets are in the closet.

Me: OK.

Ruth: The bathroom's locked. When
you need to use it, press this green
button. Someone will unlock it.

Me: Why's it locked?

Ruth: To make sure you don't purge after you eat. To make sure you're not exercising.

Me: I don't belong here. I'm not like the people here.

Ruth: I'll be back in the morning to take you to breakfast.

Me:

Ruth: I'll see you in the morning, Jake.

Me:

Ruth: This gray notebook's for you. Inside there's a feelings chart. We'll talk about the notebook and the chart during group therapy tomorrow after breakfast.

You'll meet Dr. Parker tomorrow afternoon. She's your psychiatrist.

Me: I don't need therapy. I don't belong here. I don't have an eating disorder.

Ruth: You've received a lot of information tonight. I know it's overwhelming. We'll talk more in the morning. It might help if you write down how you're feeling right now.

She leaves.

Panic, panic, panic, panic,
panic, panic, panic, panic
races and roams
through my veins.

She can't make me
share my feelings.

I don't belong here.

I won't talk to Dr. Parker.

She can't help me.

This isn't happening.

I'll throw away the notebook.
I'll shred the feelings chart.

I sit on the bed.

It isn't soft
like my bed at
Grandma's house.

I want Grandma.

I want my picture of Emily.

I repeat . . .

I'm Nobody! Who are you?
Are you — Nobody — too?

I'm Nobody! Who are you?
Are you — Nobody — too?

I'm Nobody! Who are you?
Are you — Nobody — too?

The Voice says,

YOU — ARE — REPULSIVE!

THIS NOTEBOOK BELONGS TO:

Jake

Who doesn't want to be here.

December 1996

FEELINGS CHART

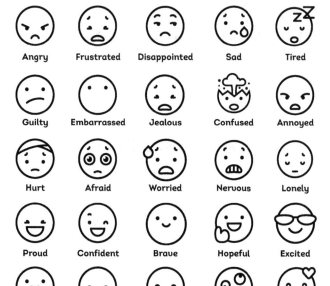

Angry Frustrated Disappointed Sad Tired

Guilty Embarrassed Jealous Confused Annoyed

Hurt Afraid Worried Nervous Lonely

Proud Confident Brave Hopeful Excited

Content Grateful Happy Silly Loved

Day 2

....

Ruth hands me a schedule.

WHISPERING PINES HOSPITAL

Jacob E. Stacey's Schedule
December 1996

Unit: Adolescent

Program: Eating Disorders

Psychiatrist: Vivian Parker, MD

Counselor: Ruth Johansen, LCPC

Dietitian: Wanda Williams, RDN, LDN, CEDRD

Art Therapist: Pedro Méndez, ATR-BC

WHISPERING PINES HOSPITAL

Monday	Tuesday	Wednesday	Thursday	Friday
9:00–9:45 Breakfast	9:00–9:45 Breakfast	9:00–9:45 Breakfast	9:00–9:45 Breakfast	9:00–9:45 Breakfast
10:00–11:00 Group Therapy	10:00–11:00 Group Therapy	10:00–11:00 Group Therapy	10:00–11:00 Group Therapy	10:00–11:00 Group Therapy
11:00–11:50 School	11:00–11:50 School	11:00–11:50 School	11:00–11:50 School	11:00–11:50 School
12:00–12:30 Meet with Dr. Parker	12:00–12:30 Free time on Adolescent Unit	12:00–12:30 Meet with Dr. Parker	12:00–12:30 Free time on Adolescent Unit	12:00–12:30 Meet with Dr. Parker
12:30–1:15 Lunch	12:30–1:15 Lunch	12:30–1:15 Lunch	12:30–1:15 Lunch	12:30–1:15 Lunch
1:30–2:15 Free time on Adolescent Unit	1:30–2:15 Art Therapy	1:30–2:15 Free time on Adolescent Unit	1:30–2:15 Art Therapy	1:30–2:15 Free time on Adolescent Unit
2:30–4:30 Group Therapy	2:30–4:30 Group Therapy	2:30–4:30 Group Therapy	2:30–4:30 Group Therapy	2:30–4:30 Group Therapy
4:45–6:00 Spend time outside, journal, read, rest	4:45–6:00 Spend time outside, journal, read, rest	4:45–6:00 Spend time outside, journal, read, rest	4:45–6:00 Spend time outside, journal, read, rest	4:45–6:00 Spend time outside, journal, read, rest
6:15–7:00 Dinner	6:15–7:00 Dinner	6:15–7:00 Dinner	6:15–7:00 Dinner	6:15–7:00 Dinner
7:15–9:00 Schoolwork, read, write	7:15–9:00 Schoolwork, read, write	7:15–9:00 Schoolwork, read, write	7:15–9:00 Schoolwork, read, write	7:15–9:00 Schoolwork, read, write

She says,

Jake, look over your schedule. Dr. Parker might check in with you more regularly than what's listed on the schedule for a while.

Starting today, you'll eat your meals with everyone who's in the eating disorders program.

I'll be back in ten minutes to take you to the cafeteria for breakfast. And I'll answer any questions you have about your schedule.

The Voice says,

RIP UP THE SCHEDULE!

YOU WON'T EAT!

SHE CAN'T MAKE YOU!

Day 2
In the Cafeteria

....

Ruth says,

*Evangeline, Belinda, Michelle, Gayle,
Jackie, and Izzy, this is Jake.*

Everyone waves.

I give an awkward wave back.

A wave people at school would laugh at.

I wait for a laugh . . .

it doesn't come.
The Voice says,

THEY'LL STILL HATE YOU.

NOBODY LIKES YOU.

NOBODY —

Ruth says,

This is your meal plan card.

She makes me
add
food
after
food
to a tray.

So.
Much.
Food.

I sit next to Izzy
and stare at
a
GIGANTIC
plate
of
calories.

I C A N N O T E A T T H I S!

Ten Minutes Later

Ruth says,

You need to eat your breakfast.

I refuse **TO EAT.**

Twenty Minutes Later

Ruth says,

Jake, group therapy starts in fifteen minutes.

I refuse **TO GO.**

Fifteen Minutes Later

Ruth says,

I'll compromise with you today. Only today.
If you eat the eggs and cereal, you can
stay on the adolescent unit as you adjust
to Whispering Pines. Tomorrow, you must
participate.

I force force force force force force force
force force force force force force force
force force force force force force force
force force force force **DOWN EGGS**
AND   CEREAL as   the   Voice
s c r e e e e e e e e e a a a a a a a a a a a a
aammmmmmmmmmmmmmmmssssssss.

Twenty Minutes Later

As Ruth walks me back
to the adolescent unit,
I can feel my
arms,
legs,
and stomach

GROWING BIGGER.

Eggs
STICK
to my ribs.

Cereal
SLIDES
around my insides.

Why
did
Mom
trick
me??????

Why
did
Mom
trap
me??????

Why
did
Mom
lock
me
away
inside
Whispering
Pines??????

She's worse than the Witch
who locks Rapunzel away
inside a hidden tower
in *Into the Woods*.

I
feel
like
I'm
locked
away
in
   A   T   O   W   E   R

Day 2
Later

....

Nurse Bruce tries to make me visit Dr.
 Parker's office.

No!

No!

Nope!

Not going to happen!

The Voice says,

DON'T TRUST DR. PARKER!

Day 3

....

Ruth knock-knock-knocks
on room 165's door.

I wish it were Grandma singing,

Rise and shine.

It's Saturday.

Are you ready for a day of F-U-N?

But Grandma's not here.

And Whispering Pines isn't F-U-N.

After breakfast, Ruth makes me attend
the eating disorders
group-therapy meeting.

Evangeline,
Belinda,
Michelle,
Gayle,
Jackie,
and Izzy
sit in a circle.

Ruth calls it a
circle of trust.

I sit
outside the circle.

I don't
trust them.

I don't
look at anyone.

I don't
share my feelings.

I sit in a chair
with my arms
crossed.

With my head
down.

Silent.

Day 4

....

Dr. Parker keeps bothering me.

She's like a gnat that won't go away.

She keeps asking me to come to her office.

I told her I'm fine.

I'm OK.

I don't belong here.

This is all a

  big,

      horrible,

            unfortunate

                  mistake.

Day 5
Will This Week Ever End?

....

Please,
Please,
Please,
Please,
Please,
Please,
Please,
Please,
Please,
Please,
Please,
Please,
Please,

let me go to Grandma's house.

I miss her red car.
I miss watching *Family Matters* and *Full
House* on Friday.
I miss her.

Day 5
Later

....

Counselor Ruth says,

Therapy is a chance to talk with someone about the things that are important to you in an effort to make your life easier, better, and more fun.

Sometimes therapy is a conversation between you and one other person. But sometimes talking about our experiences in group therapy helps.

Remember, in group therapy, we take turns. We honor everyone's experiences. We support each other.

Everyone shares.

I know she's talking about me.

Evangeline, Belinda, Michelle, Jackie,
  and Gayle share.

Izzy stares
at her arms and legs.
I know she's weighing them,
measuring every inch with her eyes.

Everyone else talks.
Everyone else shares.

I sit,
arms crossed.

I sit,
knees to chest,
trying to take up
as
little
space
as
possible,
wishing
I were
invisible.

I
don't
share.

Day 6

....

It's Saturday,
a day when I'm not forced
to sit in rooms where people
go
on
and
on
about
feelings and food.

I'm in the solarium,
a big, bright room
with tall windows,
chairs,
chaises,
couches,
tables,
puzzles.

Light floods in.

Someone taps on my shoulder.

The Voice says,

SHE FELT HOW HUGE YOU ARE!

She says,

Is anyone sitting here?

I shake my head no.

She sits in the chair near mine.

She says,

I forgot my pen in my room.

Can I borrow one of yours?

I hand her a pen.

She says,

What are you in the Pines for?

An eating disorder?

I don't know what to say.

She says,

Sorry! No offense, but you don't look like you've eaten in a while and you're pretty pale.

The Voice says,

YOU'VE EATEN TOO MUCH!

YOU COULD —

She says,

It's OK. You don't have to talk. I get it. I didn't talk for like a week after my aunt Karen dropped me off at the Pines.

That's what I call this place: The Pines.

This is my second trip to the Pines. The Pines can be scary. It gets easier. Talking and taking medicine helps me a little.

She stops talking.

She writes
words and musical notes
inside her notebook.

She writes and writes.

It looks like
songs are pouring
out of her
heart and hands.

Did Emily Dickinson
look like this
when she wrote poems?

I want to say,

I miss my Grandma.

I miss singing songs in her red car.

I miss watching —

The Voice says,

YOU ONLY NEED ME!

Day 6
Still in the Solarium

....

Thirty minutes later,
she says,

*I gotta go. My aunt Karen's here for visiting
   hours.*

Thanks for letting me borrow your pen.

*Let me know if you need any tips on how
   to survive the Pines.*

I nod my head.

She says,

By the way, I'm Kella.

She walks
toward a lady
with bright red hair.
and huge dangling earrings.

They hug
and
hug
as the earrings
S-W-A-Y.

I whisper,

You're welcome, Kella.

I'm Jake.

Day 8

Izzy
sobs
as she shares
she's gaining
TOO much weight.

I want to say,

I feel the same way.

Izzy
trembles
and
shakes
as she RUBS and RUBS
her collarbone.

I want to say,

I understand.

Counselor Ruth says,

Jake, we'd like to hear from you today.

What would happen
if I shared?

What would happen
if I told
the truth?

My truth.

Would the Voice even
let me share?

Day 8
Later

....

For the first time,
I walk behind Dr. Parker
as she leads me
from room 165
down the maze of hallways.

Her tennis shoes make a
slight squeaking sound.

Squeak-squeak-squeak.

She opens a door next to the cafeteria,
a room I hate.

She says,

Welcome to my office.

Please come in.

It's small and tidy —
like Dr. Parker.

She turns on a lamp.

There are framed photos
of what looks like her family:
two daughters, a son, and a dog.

They remind me of
the Winslows from *Family Matters*,
one of Grandma's favorite TV families.

One of our favorite shows
to watch together
on Friday nights.

Dr. Parker sits on a red chair,
a shade of red Grandma loves.

Can I trust Dr. Parker?

The Voice says,

NO!

She says,

Take a seat on the blue couch.

It looks like the couch
in the room Grandma
calls the parlor.

Grandma always says,

Jake, that isn't the family room.

It's the parlor.

It's only for entertaining guests.

I don't want to be a guest here.

I want to disappear inside the cushions.

Dr. Parker says,

Jake, how are you feeling?

She taps her pen on a clipboard:
Tap-tap-tap.

Look at your feelings chart, Jake.

Tap-tap-tap.

I ask Dr. Parker if I can call Grandma.

She says,

Most patients earn phone privileges after one week. First, you need to follow your meal plan and talk during meetings. I'm here to help you, Jake.

We sit in silence
for what feels
like a decade,
until she finally says,

Our time is up for today.

Day 9

....

Ruth, Michelle, Evangeline, Gayle,
Belinda, Jackie, Izzy, and I
sit in a circle.

We're always
sitting in circles.

I'm sick of CIRCLES

Ruth writes

I AM
POEMS

on the dry-erase board.

She says,

We're going to write I AM poems.

I think of Emily Dickinson.

I want to shout,

I'm Nobody! Who are you?

Are you — Nobody — too?

Ruth writes

    I am _____

    I wonder _____

    I understand ____

    I worry _____

    I hope _____

    I try _____

    I am _____

Everyone moves
their chairs to the table.

I'm still.

Everyone starts
write, write, writing
right away.

I'm silent.

Evangeline's pen races
                    A C R O S S
                         and
                          D
                          O
                          W
                          N
her page.

She writes with the same focus
Kella did on Saturday in the solarium.

I wonder what Kella's doing right now.

Do they sit in circles in her program?

What's the name of her program?

What does she talk about?

Music?

Michelle says,

Jake, there's room for your chair next to me. You can write your I AM poem over here. Join us.

I'm scared to share who I am.

   I'm Nobody! Who are you?

   Are you — Nobody — too?

Ruth says,

Who would like to share their I AM poem?

Evangeline's hand
SHOOTS
UP
first.

My mind wanders.
I hear
a word,
a phrase

HERE   AND   THERE.

Evangeline says,

I am Evangeline.

She wonders
why her mom
constantly criticizes
her clothes.

Michelle understands
she shouldn't throw up
after she eats.

She's too scared to stop.

140

Gayle worries
about her grades.

She's failing
French, Chemistry,
and Algebra.

                    Belinda hopes
                    her best friend
                    forgives her.

Jackie tries
to be a good daughter,
an understanding sister,
a patient friend.

She says it's hard   when she hates herself.

              Izzy passes
              as she pauses
              to rub her collarbone.

I pass, too.

Izzy and I make eye contact.

I want to say,

I get it.

141

Day 10

A nurse,
who looks allergic to smiling,
enters room 165
with a big cart.

She says,

It's time for your EKG.

*Remove your shirt and then lie down on
your bed.*

I hate feeling
exposed.

I hate
my body.

She places
COLD

142

electrodes
under
my clavicles,
on my
chest,
on my
abdomen.

All over.

She says,

You need to remain still.

I try.

I feel
itchy,
aware of
every movement,
each beat
of
my
heart.

Lub-dup.

Lub-dup.

Lub-dup.

She says,

I wish I had an eating disorder for a month.

She chuckles,
smirks.

I could lose a few pounds.

I wouldn't wish
a trip to Whispering Pines
on anyone.

Day 10
Later

....

Dr. Parker says,

Your diagnosis is bradycardia.

Your heart rate is abnormally slow because of your low weight.

Bradycardia means:

You'll use a wheelchair starting now and until your heart rate improves.

Even though you're refeeding, you're losing too much weight.

Your body's in what's called a hypermetabolic state. Your body's confused. Your metabolism is very fast.

You'll use a wheelchair until you gain more weight.

Someone will push the wheelchair for you from place to place.

Day 10
Still

....

Diagnosis:

b
   r
      a
         d
            y
               c
                  a
                    r
                      d
                         i
                           a

Izzy doesn't use a wheelchair.

I thought she was sicker than me.

Does a wheelchair make me special?

147

Night 10

....

If my pulse is so slow,
why does it feel like
    drums
beat, beat, beating
inside my chest?

Why won't the
        drummers
    stop beating?

Why won't the
        Voice
    stop talking?

It says,

YOU SAT IN A WHEELCHAIR ALL DAY!

YOU'RE NOT GETTING ANY EXERCISE!

YOU'RE GROWING BIGGER BY THE MOMENT!

I should exercise
in the bathroom.

I should run
up
and
down
the
L O N G
hallways.

Overwhelming thoughts
keep me awake
ALL
NIGHT.

Tossing,
turning,
fitfully
waiting
for
morning.

The Voice

PLAYS DRUMS
inside
my
mind:

YOU NEED ME.
I'M YOUR ONLY FRIEND.

Day 12

....

Dr. Parker says,

Jake, how are you feeling?

Tap-tap-tap.

I want to yell,

STOP TAPPING THAT STUPID PEN!

I want to yell,

I DON'T CARE TO SHARE.

I want to yell,

I HATE THIS WHEELCHAIR.

I HATE GAINING WEIGHT!

I HATE EVERYTHING!

151

Dr. Parker says,

I can tell you enjoy writing and doodling.

If you're not going to talk about your feelings with me, at least write them down in your notebook.

Maybe one day you'll share some passages during our meetings.

(I'm ignoring you, Dr. Parker.

Can you tell?)

Day 12
Later

....

**Look,
Dr. Parker!**

I'm   writing

down words.

**Look,
Counselor Ruth!**

I'm   placing

words   all   over   this

page!

Look,
Nurse Bruce!

I'm   putting

words   all   over   the

place!

A

word   HERE.

A word
THERE.

Which word should I write next
from your stupid feelings chart?

Overjoyed?

No!

Blissful?

No!

Radiant?

No!

Jovial?

No!

If

I

write

down

random

words,

will

you

leave

me

alone?

If

I

write

down

random

words,

will

YOU

stop

asking
                        how I'm feeling?

Will

YOU

think

I'm
                                  OK?

Will

YOU

think

I'm
                               FINE?

Day 15

....

Dr. Parker says,

Jake, how are you feeling?

I say,

I'm fine.

She says,

Fine *and* good *are foggy ways to express feelings.*

Look at your feelings chart.

Tap-tap-tap.

I cross my arms.

I look down.

That's **NOT** going to happen, Dr. Parker.

Day 16

....

Whispering Pines loves schedules.

They
CONTROL
our
lives.

They
try
CONTROLLING
me.

MONDAY, WEDNESDAY, FRIDAY:

Wake up,
weigh in,
shower,
stare at breakfast.

Ruth says,

Jake, you must eat!

Izzy, add milk to your cereal.

Schoolwork,
group therapy,
Dr. Parker asks too many questions,
lunch.

Ruth says,

Jake, eat the chicken!

Michelle, add the salad dressing.

Break,
group therapy,
dinner.

Ruth says,

*Jake, stop moving your food around on
    your plate.*

Izzy, add the butter.

So.
Much.
Food.

Read,
write.

Lights out!

Toss,
turn.

TUESDAY, THURSDAY:

Almost the same.

Add:
Fear foods with Wanda,
the world's strictest dietitian.

Add:
Art therapy with Pedro.

Subtract:
Time with Dr. Parker.

Add:
Jake, eat your peanut butter.

Add:
Jake, where's your feelings chart?

Add:
Izzy, please stop touching your collarbone.

EVERY DAY:

Jake, you need to use the wheelchair. Stop getting out of it.

SATURDAY:

Visiting Day. (Dr. Parker says I can have visitors soon.)

No group therapy.
No Ruth.
No Wanda!
No Dr. Parker.

(When I miss Grandma the most.)

SUNDAY:

No group therapy.
No Ruth.
No Wanda!
No Dr. Parker.

It's easier to
get away with things
on Saturday and Sunday.

There aren't as many
eyes watching my every move.

The Voice
LIKES
the
weekend.

Day 17

....

We spend
50 minutes
"at school"
most mornings.

It's a small room
with a row of dull desks
and a lonely-looking library.

Patients from different programs
"go to school"
at the same time.

Kella's here today.

She's writing inside a notebook
covered with stickers:
unicorns,
rainbows,
frogs,

cats,
dogs . . .

Ms. Denise
praises her poetry.

Izzy looks like
she's fighting
to stay awake.

She calls Nurse Bruce to get Izzy.

Focus, Jake!

Her favorite phrase
for me.

It's
hard
to
focus.

I'm tired
of being pushed
from place to place
in this wheelchair.

165

My stomach's
bloated.

My eyes
wander.

I stare at the
lonely lending library,
reading each
book's spine.

Mentally
organizing
shelves.

Arranging
books
by size.

Focus, Jake!

Mentally
adding
titles.

Arranging
books
by color.

Focus, Jake!

Mentally
removing
titles.

Someone keeps
adding joke books.

Focus, Jake!

Joke books with
colorful spines.

Joke books with
exciting titles.

Joke books like the ones Ms. Wozny,
my fourth-grade teacher,
loved to share.

Will I ever laugh
at school again?

Focus, Jake!

I wish this were
a notebook
to record jokes,
to record
pages
and
pages
and
pages
of
hilarious
jokes.

Knock, knock.
Who's there?

Focus, Jake!

Focus!

Focus!

Focus!

Day 19

....

Dr. Parker says, *Your heart rate improved. You don't need to use the wheelchair anymore.*

The Voice says,

THIS MEANS YOU'RE NOT THE SICKEST PATIENT IN THE EATING DISORDERS PROGRAM ANYMORE!

Dr. Parker says,

Now that you've been here for two weeks and you're doing a better job following your meal plan, I'm giving you phone and Visiting Day privileges. Your mom and grandma are going to visit on Saturday. Is that OK?

I say,

Yes!

Inside,
it almost
feels like I'm smiling.

I'm going to see Grandma.

Day 20

Mom looks like
she hasn't slept
in a week.

There's more
gray than brown
in her hair.

She looks
older,
less like herself,
worn.

Me: Where's Grandma?

Mom: Your grandma isn't feeling well.
I'm worried about her. I'm worried about
you. I'm worried about everything.

Typical.

Mom brings
worry everywhere
she goes.

We stare at each other.

Neither knows
what to say.

Mom: Your dad and I miss you.

Silence.

Mom: You look a little better.

The Voice yells,

SHE MEANS YOU'RE GAINING WEIGHT.

She pulls a
yellow note
out of her purse.

Grandma's
fancy handwriting
stares at me.

Mom: Can I read aloud this note from
your grandma?

I nod.

Mom clears her throat.

I think about what Ms. Burns always
    said
before I read aloud her mysteries at the
    Tinley Terrace:

Reading aloud is love.

My Dearest Jake,

I'm sorry I couldn't visit today. I miss you.

Mom pauses.

She wipes away a tear.

This note is to remind you, you have your whole life to live. You can beat this thing if you try. Give yourself permission to eat. Love yourself. You can put it behind you, and start to go forward. Give yourself permission to try.

Please take care of my boy.
I love you to the moon and back!

Your grandma

Silence.

Mom and I stare at each other.

Reading aloud is love —
is writing love, too?

The Voice says,

That's a lie.

Those are all big lies!

NOBODY LOVES YOU!

Day 20
Later

....

After Mom leaves, I
reread
and
reread
and
reread
Grandma's note in the solarium.

Someone taps on my shoulder.

Kella: How did it feel to have a visitor?

Me: Disappointing.

She looks surprised I talked.

Kella: Why?

Me: My grandma was supposed to visit.
Saturday's always our day.

Kella: Sorry. That sucks.

What do you and your grandma usually do on Saturday?

The Voice says,

STOP TALKING!
YOU CANNOT TRUST PEOPLE HERE!

Me: We.
      Will she laugh at me?
Me: We.
     Will she make fun of me?

Me: We shop. We watch movies. We listen to musicals.

      She doesn't laugh.

Kella: Music's my life. Seriously. Sometimes it's the only reason I get out of bed. I write my own songs. Some of my friends think I'm too intense about music, but I don't care. What's your favorite musical?

Me: *Into the Woods.*

Kella: I've never heard of it. I'll look for it at the Nichols Library after I get out of the Pines. I walk by it every day on my way home from Naperville Central. The library and Anderson's Bookshop are my two favorite places in Naperville.

      She doesn't make fun of me.

I want to tell Kella
about every scene of *Into the Woods*,
about Little Red Riding Hood,
about Jack's cow and the Baker's beans,
but the VOICE is angry and so loud.

S C C R R R E E E E E E E E E E E E E E E E E E E E E E E E E
C C C C C C C C C C H H H H H H H H H H H H H H H H H H H
S C R E E E E E E E E E E E E E E E E E E E E E E E E E E E
A A A A A A A A A A A A A A A A A A A A A A A M M M M M
M M M M M M M M M M M M M M M M M M M M M M M
S C R E E E E E E E E E E E E E E E E E E E E E E E E E E C C
C C C C C C C C C C C C C C C H H H H H H H H H H H H H H

Day 22

....

Dr. Parker: Jake, how are you feeling?

Me: Your question scares me.

Dr. Parker: Why does it scare you?

Dr. Parker: Take as much time as you need.

Me: I don't know.

Me: Maybe because it **forces** me to deal.

Dr. Parker: Deal? What does that mean?

Me:

It . . .

It means . . .

It means I'll . . .

It means I'll deal . . .

It means I'll deal with . . .

PAI

N!

It . . .

It means . . .

It means I'll . . .

It means I'll deal . . .

It means I'll deal with . . .

CONF

USION

Me: I don't know what it all means.

Dr. Parker: One of your treatment goals is to develop relationships with people your own age. Talking about it could help you better connect with other teens and express your feelings in real life.

Jake, you may feel calmer, better, and more at ease.

Jake, it could help you figure   it all out.

Jake, it could help you   start to heal.

Jake,   how do you feel right now?

Jake,   breathe in. Breathe out.

Jake,   count to ten.

Jake,   take as much time as you need.

Jake . . .

Jake . . .

Jake . . .

Jake . . .

Jake . . .

Jake, what do **YOU** need?

What do I need?

What do I need?

What do I need?

I don't know.

I'm tired.

I'm scared.

I miss my grandma.

Why didn't she come see me?
Is she ashamed of me?

Day 23

....

Fine!

OK!

I'm not ready to talk about it out loud.

I'll try writing it all down.

Maybe I'll share some of it with Dr. Parker.

At least she doesn't
tap-tap-tap her pen
when I do what she wants.

Once upon a time,
I felt happy —
carefree,
big smiles,
loving,

full of hope.

Happiest with Grandma.

I always walk a
little lighter,
breathe a little easier
when I'm with her.

When she's beside me.

Friday afternoon trips to
Venture Department Store to buy
books, clothes, anything I wanted.

Saturday morning trips to
Walt's Food Center for samples —
little plastic cups filled with
spicy chicken strips and
mint chocolate chip ice cream and
steaming hot pizza rolls.

Before I feared food.

Saturday evening trips to
Blockbuster Video to rent
marvelous musicals
starring:

♫ Judy Garland in *The Wizard of Oz* ♫

♫ Julie Andrews in *The Sound of Music* ♫

♫ Joanna Gleason in *Into the Woods* . . . ♫

Sunday morning trips to
the public library for
stacks
of
books.

Make sure you take care of my boy!

Something Grandma
says only to me.

Safe,
loved,
happy.

190

Day 25

....

Dr. Parker says,

Write more.

Grandma bought me
Goofy's Big Race
from the grocery store
when I was six or seven.

She used a coupon.

Slow and steady,
steady and slow,
that's the way to go.

I asked her to read it aloud
over
and
over
and

over
again.

Until I memorized it.

Slow and steady,
steady and slow,
that's the way to go.

Until it crawled inside my heart
and rested there.

Grandma reminded me to
Slow down.
Breathe.
Take it all in.
Calm down.
Remember Goofy.
Remember to

Take care of my boy!

He's safe.

He's loved.

He's happy.

Day 26

....

Kella seems sad in the solarium.

It doesn't look like
songs are
playing inside
her head.

She doesn't look like
a musical.

She doesn't look
full of songs.

Is she OK?

Kella catches me staring.

She says,

Hey!

I've had a ROUGH day.

Life SUCKS sometimes.
                    I nod.

I gotta get out of THE PINES.

*I gotta get back to school, but I'm so, so,
so, so, so, so, so sad today. I can't shake it.*
                    I nod.

I'm going for a walk. See ya later.
                    I nod.

The Voice screams,

**WE
GOTTA
GET
OUT
OF
HERE,
TOO!**

Day 26
Later

....

I write Kella a note.

I rip it up.

I write Kella another note.

I rip it up.

I write Kella yet another note.

I rip it up.

I write Kella **YET ANOTHER** note.

Will Kella think I'm strange if I give her
a note?

Hi, Kella,
I hope a walk helped calm you down.
You didn't look like a musical today. You
usually remind me of how I feel when I
see Barbra Streisand in *Hello, Dolly!*

Today, you looked the way I feel when
   I'm at school.

Sad.
Alone.
Suffocating.

I wonder,
do you feel like I do at school?

Jake,
from the blue couch in the solarium

The Voice says,

RIP IT UP!

RIIIIIIIIIIIIIIIIIIIIIIIIIIIIIIIIIIIIII
IIIIIIIIIIIIIIIIIIIIIIIIIIIIIIIIIIIIIIII
IIIIIIIIIIIIIIIIIIIIIIIIIIIIIIIIIIIIIIII
IIIIIIIIIIIIIIIIIIIIIIIIIIIIIIIIIIIIP!

Day 30

....

Wanda wears
high heels
I can hear
clack-clack-clacking
from a mile away.

The clacking means
she and her
BIG binder
are on the way to room 165.

To me.

Wanda's ready to weigh me.

Remove your shoes.

Teeth Teeth Teeth Teeth
chatter. chatter. chatter. chatter.

Take off your hoodie.

Palms Palms Palms Palms
sweat. sweat. sweat. sweat.

Remove everything from your pockets.

Heart Heart Heart Heart
races. races. races. races.

Step backward on the balance-beam scale.

Shoulders Shoulders Shoulders Shoulders
slump. slump. slump. slump.

Don't turn around.

Teeth chatter. Teeth chatter. Teeth chatter. Teeth chatter.

Palms sweat. Palms sweat. Palms sweat. Palms sweat.

Heart races. Heart races. Heart races. Heart races.

Shoulders slump. Shoulders slump. Shoulders slump. Shoulders slump.

Teeth chatter. Teeth chatter. Teeth chatter. Teeth chatter.

Palms sweat. Palms sweat. Palms sweat. Palms sweat.

Heart races. Heart races. Heart races. Heart races.

Shoulders slump. Shoulders slump. Shoulders slump. Shoulders slump.

Teeth chatter. Teeth chatter. Teeth chatter. Teeth chatter.

Palms sweat. Palms sweat. Palms sweat. Palms sweat.

Day 30
Still

....

Wanda opens her
big binder.

She updates
my meal plan.

She adds
1 fat,
1 ounce of protein,
1 peanut butter packet,
1 cup of this,
1 tablespoon of that.

Always
1 more.

Never
1 less.

As she talks and
talks and talks
and talks and talks
about facing fear foods,

as she talks and
talks and talks
and talks and talks
about vitamins
A, E, D, and K,

all I hear
are the sounds from
today's weigh-in.

I hear the
clunk, clunk, clunk
of the big
sliding weight.

I hate,

I detest,

I despise

that sound.

I hear the
tick, tick, tick
of the small
sliding weight.

I loathe

clunk, clunk, clunk,
tick, tick, tick,

clunk, clunk, clunk,
tick, tick, tick.

I abhor

clunk, clunk, clunk,
tick, tick, tick,

clunk, clunk, clunk,
tick, tick, tick.

I hate

those sounds.

Clunk, clunk, clunk,
tick, tick, tick.

Clunk, clunk, clunk,
tick, tick, tick.

I want to
SCREAM.

I want to
RUN AWAY
from Wanda
and her
big binder.

I want to
CRY.

Day 30
In the Afternoon

....

Ruth walks us from
fear foods to art therapy.

The walls are painted
green, purple, and blue.

Pedro calls them
calming colors.

He doesn't
arrange chairs
in a circle.

We each have a space,
a spot to create.

Pedro says,

Hi, Jake!

His voice is
gentle.

He always wears fun ties.

Cats and unicorns are
dancing together today.

A half-smile slips out.

Pedro passes out paper lunch bags
with purple strips of paper
paper-clipped on the outside.

The paper smells like a library.

On a massive chalkboard, Pedro writes

Draw a self-portrait on the paper
lunch bag.

You can use any of the art supplies on
the yellow table.

Write words on the strips of paper that
represent you.

Put the strips inside your bag.

Izzy and I look at each other.

I see terror in Izzy's eyes.

She rubs her collarbone.

I feel like I'm going to throw up.

The Voice yells,

TAPE TOGETHER TEN BAGS.

**THAT'S THE ONLY WAY YOUR
SELF-PORTRAIT WILL FIT.**

My half-smile disappears.   I disappear
                              inside myself.

Day 31

....

Ruth says,

Tell us about a time you were happy.

Evangeline talks about her
seventh birthday party.

She says,

*My mom let me wear what I wanted. There
were so many balloons. Bouquets of
balloons in multiple colors. Yellow. Green.
Purple . . .*

Evangeline's bouquet of balloons
reminds me of
*Joseph and the Amazing Technicolor
   Dreamcoat,*
a musical Grandma loves.

Evangeline looks so happy
as she goes
on
and
on
and
on
about
happy
times
with
friends
and
balloons.

Is Evangeline getting better?

I wish I could talk like —

The Voice says,

YOU BETTER NOT BE WEAK LIKE HER!

Izzy's family owns a plant nursery in Niles.

She says,

I'm happy when I'm in the middle of a garden.
Growing tomatoes is a family tradition.

She doesn't normally talk this much.

Izzy says,

Growing tomatoes is the only time I feel —

She stops talking about tomatoes
    to
  r u b
her right collarbone.

Will Izzy ever stop rubbing her collarbones?

Michelle smiles
as she reminisces
about going to New York City.

She says,

*I spent five days in New York City. I saw
five musicals and visited two museums.
I want to do it again one day.*

Will I ever see a musical on Broadway
  with Grandma?

Just Grandma and me!

Me and Grandma in
N
Y
C!

Ruth says,

Jake, would you like to share?

I say,

I

.

.

.

No.

Evangeline says,

When were you happy, Jake?
Come on.

Share with us.

I say,

I was happy —

The Voice says,

RUTH AND DR. PARKER KEEP TELLING YOU
TALKING HELPS!

YOU DON'T WANT TO GET BETTER.

IF YOU GET BETTER, IT MEANS YOU'RE NOT —

Evangeline says,

Come on, Jake!

Share.

I just stare.

Evangeline
looks
disappointed.

I
disappoint
everyone.

Day 31
Later

....

I lie in bed
replaying the day
over and over again.

What I wanted to share with Evangeline
  is . . .

Every Saturday when I was little,
I ran to the door
that leads from
Grandma's dining room
to the garage.

I'd open the door and

S H O U T,

  Good morning, beautiful red car.

  Hello, friend!

One day, I'll drive Grandma around
town.

We'll sing "Giants in the Sky."

There are giants in the sky!
There are big, tall, terrible, awesome,
scary, wonderful
Giants in the sky!

I'd close the dining room door,
a huge smile on my face.

Day 33

....

Dr. Parker says,

Jake, write down some more memories.

We'll talk about them during our next session.

Everything changed in seventh grade.

Loser.

            Wimp.

                        Freak.

Words that
tattooed
hate,
fear,
sadness

on my
heart.

All words meant to bring me

D

O

W

N.

All words meant to

L

O

W

E

R

me.

All words meant to show I was

L

E

S

S

E

R

than,
not as GREAT.

I
believed the people
saying the words.

Actually,

I
still
do.

Day 33
Later

....

Frieden,
I'm
broken.

Day 34

....

Kella looks like a musical again.

She's write-write-writing lyrics
in her stickered notebook.

I can almost see musical notes
　　　F L Y I N G
out of her hands and heart again.

She stops writing and says,

Hey, Jake!

Me: Hi.

Kella: Sorry for being so grouchy last
week.

Me: You weren't.

Kella: I know I was. This week was much better.

Me: I'm glad you're feeling better.

I think about the note I wrote her.

I wish I hadn't ripped it up.

It's easier for me to write than to talk.

Kella: My aunt Karen should be here soon. I'm getting out of the Pines today.

Kella's leaving?

Really?

Who will I sit with in the solarium?

Kella: I gotta go pack up my stuff.

Me: That's good. Good luck with your music.

Kella: I'm gonna check out *Into the Woods* from the Nichols Library next week.

I smile.

Kella: Bye.

Me: Goodbye.

> I feel like crying.

Kella turns around and says,

You're gonna conquer your eating disorder.

I believe in you.

You'll feel joy one day.

The Voice says,

YOU —

Me: I —

The Voice says,

YOU ARE —

Me: I hope —

Kella walks away.

Is this what it feels like to have a friend?

Day 35

Evangeline was

D
I
S
C
H
A
R
G
E
D

T
O
D
A
Y!

I wish I were, too.

Day 36

Enter the cafeteria.

Day
after
day.

Pick up a tray.

Day
after
day.

Pick up a
meal plan card.

Day
after
day.

A card,
a plan,
dictated,
decided,
designed by Wanda
and her big binder.

The Voice
inside my head
is still so
LOUD.

It says,

YOU'RE A BIG DISAPPOINTMENT!

It says,

YOU DON'T DESERVE FOOD!

It says,

YOU BETTER NOT EAT 3 OUNCES OF PROTEIN!

It says,

YOU'RE DISGUSTING!

It says,

PUT BACK THOSE TWO STARCHES!

It says . . .

        It says . . .

                It says . . .

Day
after
day.

      Day
      after
      day.

            Day
            after
            day.

                  Day
                  after
                  day.

What if I yelled,

Shut up,
VOICE!

What if I demanded,

Leave me alone,
VOICE!

What if I screamed,

Be quiet,
VOICE!

What if . . .

Day 38

....

Dr. Parker turns on her lamp.

She says,

Take a seat on the blue couch, Jake!

Now that you've been refeeding your brain for a while, we're ready to conduct some psychological tests.

She holds up
what she calls
inkblots.

What do you see here?

How about here?

Question.
After.
Question.

I can barely
keep my eyes open.

Dr. Parker reads
scenarios off cards.

It feels like we're playing
the world's longest and cruelest
game of Trivial Pursuit.

She tells me to respond with . . .

Very Often

Often

Sometimes

Rarely

Never

Question.
After.
Question.

I
want
to
sleep.

zzz
        zzz
                zzz
                        zzz
                                zzz

Dr. Parker reads
problems
off
a
paper.

She asks
if I'm bothered
by any of them.

She tells me to respond with . . .

Not at all

Several days

More than half the days

Nearly every day

Question.
After.
Question.

So.
Many.
Questions.

Day 38
Later

....

Dr. Parker says,

Jake, our conversations have been helping give us some answers. They're not the same as the answers you'll find for yourself, but they helped give us names for some of the things you're dealing with. We've known you've been suffering with anorexia nervosa since you were admitted.

In addition to anorexia nervosa, it seems like you're dealing with several different diagnoses all at once, so we'll talk about all of them to help you understand.

Diagnosis:
Depression

Diagnosis:
Obsessive-
Compulsive
Disorder
(OCD)

Day 38
Still

....

My head spins as
Dr. Parker explains
each diagnosis.

I can see my
obsessive and
compulsive
behaviors.

I count calories.

I memorize nutritional information.

There are repetitive thoughts
inside my head,
playing on repeat.

I have strict,
necessary
rituals with food at home.

I won't write those down.

I won't admit them to Dr. Parker.

Dr. Parker says,

Anorexia nervosa and depression often go together.

As you continue feeding your brain, we can work on the underlying issues.

You can —

The Voice interrupts,

STOP FEEDING YOUR BRAIN.

YOU ONLY NEED ME.

Day 40

....

I'm taking three new medications.

Eyes = hard to keep open

Head = throbbing

Throat = sore

Stomach = bloated,
          bloated,
              bloated,
                  bloated,

SOOooOOOOOOOOOOOoooOOOOOO
OOOOOOOOOO

BLOATED.

Day 43

........·····

Ruth says,

*Share a time you helped someone or
  something.*

Everyone
starts
sharing.

Izzy saved a
baby bunny
in her parents' garden.

Michelle performed
CPR on a stranger.

A memory pops
into my mind.

Before I can stop myself,
I say,

I stole a dog in the second grade.

I saw him every day
on the way home
from school.

He was
tied up
outside.

He looked
sad,
angry,
lonely.

Woof! (Please rescue me.)

Woof! Woof! (They're mean to me.)

Woof! Woof! Woof! (Take me home.)

Pleading with me.

I rescued a dog in the second grade.

Everyone stares.

Ruth says,

Tell us more.

I say,

No!

That's enough.

Michelle rolls her eyes.

Day 43
Later

....

As everyone's leaving group therapy,
Ruth stops me and says,

Jake, will you share the rest of your story?

She's surprised
when I say,

I'll write down the story tonight.

Maybe I'll let you read it tomorrow.

Day 44

I let Ruth read this version of the story:

The dog,
who I named Jessie,
snuggled inside my coat.

I pedaled my bike,
the one with the
blue banana seat,
faster
and
faster.

Pedal.
Pedal.
Pedal.

Pedaling

U

P

a

hill,

D

O

W

N

a

hill.

Pedal.
Pedal.
Pedal.

U

P

a

hill,

D

O

W

N

a

hill.

Faster.

Faster.

Moving toward home.

Pedal.
Pedal.
Pedal.

Losing my grip . . .

I broke . . .

I bruised . . .

I betrayed . . .

I dropped . . .

a dog in the second grade.

Jessie
whined,
whimpered,
howled
in pain.

Jessie cried
and
cried
and
cried.

Did I kill him trying to help?

I panicked.

I froze.

I carefully picked him up.

I carefully placed him inside my coat.

Z
I
P

I felt his gentle heart
beating
FAST
against my
chest.

Beat.

Beat.

Beat.

I felt his body

shaking.

Shake.

Shake.

Shake.

Pedaling toward
home.

Pedaling toward
hope.

Pedaling toward
help.

A kind
veterinarian
put
Jessie
back
together
again.

I saw him two weeks later.

Tied up
outside.

He looked
sad,
angry,
lonely.

I failed him.

I found a different
route home
from school.

One where I
didn't see him.

One where I
couldn't feel
his pain.

Day 44
Later

....

Ruth: Thanks for letting me read the story about Jessie. It must have been hard to see a dog howling in pain when you were trying to help.

Me: Yes!

Ruth: You were trying to protect him. You were compassionate.

Do you sometimes feel the same feelings you thought Jessie felt?

Me: I don't know.

The Voice says,

DON'T TRUST HER.

Ruth: Jake, everyone here wants to help you — the same way you wanted to help the dog.

The Voice says,

SHE'S LYING.

Ruth: The negative voice inside your head doesn't help you. It hurts you. It makes you sad and angry. It traps you like Jessie was. It wants —

The Voice says,

SHE'S TRYING TO TRICK YOU.

I tune her out.

Day 50

.... ·····

I
miss
Grandma
EXTRA
hard
today.

I ask Bruce if I can call Grandma.

He says,

Yes! Give me a few minutes.

I wait until he says,

*Your grandma's not home. She's not
answering the phone.*

I wanted to tell Grandma how much
I miss our Saturday night traditions.

Traditions before the Voice took over.
Saturday nights meant . . .

   1. A new episode of
     The Golden Girls.

   2. An ice cream sundae
     with an extra cherry
          on
          top.

We
laughed
until
we
cried.

I wanted to say,

Grandma,
I wish I could
eat an ice cream sundae
with
Dorothy,

Rose,
Blanche,
Sophia, and
YOU.

1. Ice cream is a
   fear food.

2. I don't remember
   what it feels like to
   laugh. :(

Day 51

....

The new medications
are helping
a little.
I can focus more,
even if
the pill for
OCD
makes
me
S
O
O
O
O
O
O
O
O
O
sleepy.

Day 54

....

Dr. Parker says,

Write about a time you stood up for
yourself or someone else.

I close my eyes.

I'm ten years old again.

I see myself
playing school
in my bedroom.

There's a piece of chalk
in one hand
and a copy of Disney's *Beauty and the*
Beast Novelization
in the other.

I teach
imaginary students
about the characters

Belle,
       Mrs. Potts,
              Chip,
                        Beast.

I draw
each character
on a chalkboard.

In a dramatic voice,
I say,

Attention, students!

Students, attention!

Please draw each character inside your
   purple notebook.

I bump into my waterbed —
that awful,
oversize
waterbed
Mom and Dad
bought me without asking if I wanted it —

as I
walk around
the room,
checking in on
imaginary students.

I want
to toss
it
OUT
the
window.

I call Mom
to my bedroom
before I have
a meltdown.

Me: My waterbed takes up too much
space. I need more space for my
classroom.

Mom: It's your bedroom. Your students
are imaginary.

Me: Can I have a regular bed?

Mom: No. We spent a lot of money
on it. You're lucky to have a waterbed.
Sometimes you're so ungrateful.

Mom leaves.

Who thought a bed filled with water was
   a good idea?

I walk over to my
big brown desk.

Three drawers on the
                    RIGHT.

Three drawers on the
LEFT.

One BIG drawer
in
the
MIDDLE.

260

I pull out the
top drawer,
the one
with
scissors
inside.

I walk over to the bed.

STAB.

STAB.

STAB.

Water flows to the

RIGHT.

Water flows to the

LEFT.

Problem solved.

Now my students have

S   P   A   C   E.

Now my students will be happy

LIKE I WAS IN
MS. WOZNY'S CLASS.

Day 54
Later

....

I can still hear Dad yelling,

JAKE!!!!!!!

WHAT DID YOU DO?

YOU FLOODED YOUR BEDROOM
  AND THE HALLWAY!!!

YOU RUINED THE CARPET!

WHAT THE HELL IS WRONG
  WITH YOU?

YOU HAVE NO COMMON SENSE!

HAVE YOU LOST YOUR MIND?

He wouldn't
look at me

or talk to me
for a month.

BUT did I get a new bed?

Yes!

Yes,
I did!

One with springs
and full of cotton.

Day 57

....

Dr. Parker: Jake, did you write about a time you stood up for yourself or someone else?

Me: Yes.

Dr. Parker: Do you feel comfortable reading it aloud?

Me: No.

Dr. Parker: What if you pretend you're reading it aloud to your grandma? I know how much you miss her. I know how much you love her.

I think about what Ms. Burns told me at the Tinley Terrace:

Reading aloud is love.

Is Dr. Parker
trying to
trick me?

Even if she's
trying to trick me,
I miss Grandma.

I miss reading aloud to Ms. Burns.

Reading aloud is love.

I clear my
throat.

I take a
deep breath.

I pretend
Grandma and Ms. Burns
are beside me.

I pretend
I'm holding their
soft hands.

I read aloud
the story
about *that*
dreadful
waterbed.

Dr. Parker says,

Thank you for sharing, Jake.

I'm proud of you.

*It's interesting you wanted your students,
even if they're imaginary, to have enough
space.*

*When will you give yourself permission to
take up space?*

Day 58

I freeze in place
as a
scanning arm
passes slowly
OVER
my
body.

Measuring
the density
of my
hip.

Measuring
the density
of my
spine.

Measuring
the density
of me.

Day 58
Still

....

Diagnosis:

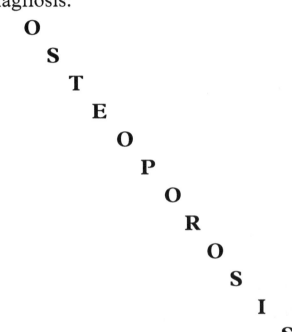

O
S
T
E
O
P
O
R
O
S
I
S

Wanda opens her big binder and says,

Jake, you'll add more calcium and vitamin D to your meal plan. Your body needs these vitamins to protect your bones. It isn't too late to prevent further damage.

Day 58
Later

. . . .

Frieden,
I'm destroying my bones.

Frieden,
I want to protect my bones,
but I don't.

Frieden,
I'm being pulled apart inside . . .

DO THIS!!!
    NO, DO THIS!
        NO! NO! NO!
           DO THIS . . .

Frieden,
my brain confuses me.

Frieden,
I don't know
what to do.

Day 64

....

Izzy shares
how she feels
calm and safe
when she works in
her parents' nursery in Niles.

She talks about growing vegetables
more than the Witch talks about
rutabaga, arugula, and rampion
in *Into the Woods*.

Izzy describes her
Carefree Sunshine roses.

Blah.

Blah.

Blah.

I tune everyone out.

My mind wanders
back to when it all began.

I threw up in the closet, Mom!

My stomach hurts.

I have a fever.

I don't feel well.

My throat hurts.

I couldn't sleep.

Please, please
let me stay home alone
from school
one more day.

All lies.

Lies to avoid being
bullied.
Lies to avoid
teasing
and
tormenting.

Lies to avoid
verbal stones.

Stones that helped create the Voice.

Stones that gave the Voice permission to
  speak.

Safe in my bedroom
with never-before-used
office supplies,
stored in the third drawer
                    on the right:

          fluorescent highlighters,
            chalk, pens, pencils,
            paper clips, staples,
          sticky notes of every color.

Safe in my bedroom
with piles of books.
Books that calmed me,
characters who knew me.

Safe in my bedroom
with daytime talk show hosts
who told me about the world.

Safe in my bedroom
smiling,
laughing,
singing
along with
Fraggle Rock,
dancing
my
cares
away.

Safe in my bedroom
on a small bed,
a bed filled with
cotton and coils.

I loved those days,
home alone in my bedroom.

Days when I felt the way
I did during the weekend
with Grandma.

Days when I felt calm
while Mom and Dad were away.

Safe . . .

Ruth says,

Jake, it's your turn to share.

I say,

What was the question?

                      Everyone rolls their eyes.

I don't share.

Day 64
Still

....

Frieden, why am I so angry?

Frieden, why am I so sad?

Frieden, why am I so

U

G

H?

Day 65

Izzy looks like
she's been awake
for a month.

The bags
under her eyes
are puffy,
swollen.

She refuses
breakfast.

She refuses
lunch.

She refuses
EVERYTHING.

She
rubs
her
collarbones
raw.

I
wish
I
could
help
her,
even
if
I
can't
help
myself.

Day 66

Izzy left last night
for an eating disorders program
on a ranch with horses.

I wonder what Izzy's doing right now.

Probably telling a horse about her
    Carefree Sunshine roses.

Maybe the horses
will tell her to stop
rubbing her collarbones.

Maybe horses could help me.

Day 69

....

Bruce says,

*Your mom and grandma are waiting for you
    in the solarium.*

Grandma's here?

    I

           j

        u

             m

                p

out   **of**   **bed.**

My
heart
lights
up.

I
power
walk
down
the
maze
of
hallways.

My
eyes
D A R T
around
the
busy
solarium.

I spot Mom and
Grandma's
favorite
red sweater.

I wave.
She looks different.

She looks sick,
fragile.

Like she might break.

Mom and Grandma sing,
"Happy Birthday to You" in unison.

Wait!

It's my birthday?

I never know the date in Whispering
Pines.

Mom says,

Happy, happy fourteenth birthday!
I'll leave you two alone for a while.

I sit
on
a
big

blue
chair
beside
Grandma.

She hands me a
bright red package
and says,

Give your old grandma a BIG smooch.

I kiss her cheek.

She says,

*Now you can open your present from your
    mom and me!*

I remove
a big red bow
and unwrap
the brightest red wrapping paper.

I open a box
and stare down at
pastels,
pens,
colored pencils,
markers,
and a sketchbook.

She says,

You've always loved office supplies.

*I know you'll create something special with
them.*

I say,

You're right.

They're perfect.

Day 69
Twenty Minutes Later

The solarium's quiet.

Everyone's gone except
Grandma and me.

Grandma says,

There are so many things I miss.

*I miss how you loved swimming almost
every afternoon in the summer.*

*I miss celebrating your birthday at Daniel's
Restaurant in Orland Park.*

There are so many things I'll miss.

Grandma starts crying.

Bruce says,

Visiting time ends in five minutes.

I say,

I'm sorry, Grandma.

I'll work harder.

I'll try.

I hope I can come home soon.

Day 69
Five Minutes Later

....

I walk Grandma
to the locked door.

I wish she could stay.

I wish I could say,

Grandma,
this door

           blocks me
      from the outside world.

I wish I could say,

Grandma,
this door

               separates me
              from the living.
She presses the doorbell.

Nurse Bruce buzzes her out.

As the door closes,
she says,

*Happy fourteenth birthday, my dear
  grandbaby!*

Remember, take care of my boy.

I love you to the moon and back again.

I say,

I'll take care of your boy.

I love you to the moon and back.

I love you with my whole heart.

We pinky wave,
the way we've
said goodbye
since I was five.

Day 69
Ten Minutes Later

....

Frieden,
Grandma
wobbled
as
I
watched
her
walk
away.

Frieden,
I
think
I
lied
when
I
said
I'd
try.

Frieden,
I'm
worried
about
her.

Please
help
her.

Please
bless
her.

Please
protect
her.

Day 75
Afternoon

....

People come,
        people go
                at
                    Whispering Pines.

Sara's the newest.

I wish she would GO.

She does everything Ruth asks.

She follows all the rules.

Sara says,

Jake doesn't even try.

He wants to be the sickest person here.

He wants all the attention.

292

Butterflies
flit and fly
around
inside
my stomach
as Sara shares
the truth about me.

I want to be the sickest,
but I also want to go home.

What if I trick them?

What if I pretend like I'm doing better?

What if I play a part in a play?

The Voice is confused.

I'm confused.

Who's in control?

Is   the   Voice   really   me?

Day 78

....

Sara tosses me
UNDER
a big bus
during
group therapy.

Again.

The butterflies in my stomach are back,
and this time they brought bees.

Sara thinks she knows everything.

Here are four facts she brings up
ALL THE TIME:

1. She's seventeen.

2. She graduated from high school at
   sixteen.

3. She's an English major at Northwest-
ern University.

4. She's from Oak Brook.

She thinks she's the
  QUEEN
of group therapy.

She thinks she's the
  MAYOR
of Whispering Pines.

Sara says,

He brings us all down by not trying.

I want to YELL at the TOP OF MY
  VOICE,

BUZZZZZZZZZZZZZZZZZZZ
ZZZZZZZZZZZZZZZZZZZZZ
ZZZZZZZZZZZZZZZZZZZZZ
ZZZZZZZZZZZZZZZZZZZZZ

OFF!

Day 79

....

I
try,
try,
try
to act like the "good teen"
everyone wants me to be.

During group therapy,
Ruth says,

Jake, thank you for sharing today.

Day 82

....

I
pretend,
pretend,
pretend

I'm interested
when Dr. Parker talks about
what she thinks are my
"underlying issues."

Dr. Parker says,

Thank you for talking about how you're
feeling.

Day 86

I
imagine,
imagine,
imagine

I'm an actor in a play.

I say the lines
everyone wants to hear.

During fear foods,
Wanda says,

Thank you for participating today.

Day 87
....

How much longer can I pretend?

How much longer can I play this game?

How much longer until Dr. Parker says
    I can go home?

Day 89
....

Today's
Sara's
last day in
group therapy.

She's finally buzzing off.

She met her goals.

She reached her target weight.

Everyone says,

Well done, Sara!!!!

Bravo, Sara!!!

You rock, Sara!!!

Sara!!! Sara!!! Sara!!!

I glare at her.
Later, I say to Dr. Parker,

I've been here
for almost
ninety days.

It feels like
everyone gets
discharged
except me.

Dr. Parker says,

*I can see you're trying. You're almost ready
to move from the inpatient program to
the outpatient program. This means your
family will drive you here in the morning
and you'll go home in the evening.*

We'll talk more about this plan in a week or so.

My plan worked.

It really worked.

Day 94

....

Dr. Parker says,

Jake, you'll transfer from the inpatient program to the outpatient program next Monday.

You'll stay in the same group therapy.

You'll come here Monday through Friday from nine a.m. to six p.m.

You need to follow your meal plan at home on Saturday and Sunday.

You can do it.

You're ready.

What questions do you have for me?

I say,

I don't have any questions.

I'm ready to go home.

Day 94
Later

....

I lied to
Dr. Parker.

Dr. Parker,
I'm not ready.

You shouldn't
trust me.

I don't
trust myself.

I want to go home
to restrict,
to lose weight.

I've been
playing
a game,
a part in a play.

I need
control of
my body
again.

The Voice
helps me
manipulate you.

It manipulates
everything,
everyone.

Day 99
Monday

....

I pack up
everything
in room 165.

Mom
meets me
in the lobby.

She says,

Jake, you look good.

I
feel
like
throwing up
all
over
the
lobby.

What I hear is,

Jake, you gained tons of weight!

I
feel
like
screaming.

What I hear is,

Jake, you no longer look like you have an
  eating disorder!

306

Outpatient
Night 1
Monday

Home
feels
unfamiliar.

Outpatient
Day 2
Tuesday Morning

As Mom pulls into
Whispering Pines' parking lot
to drop me off,
I say I want to stay
at Grandma's house tonight.

She looks like she's
holding back buckets of tears.

Mom: I wasn't sure when to tell you . . .

.

.

.

Mom: You're already dealing with a lot.

Her voice sounds shaky.

It scares me.

Mom: Your grandma's in the hospital.

It feels like
a giant STOMPS on my heart.

Me: Why didn't you tell me??? For how long????

Mom: She's been in the hospital for three weeks.

Me: I want to see Grandma tonight.

Mom: I don't think that's a good idea.

Me: I NEED TO SEE HER! SHE'S MY FAVORITE PERSON!

.

.

.

Mom winces.

I think this fact
    STINGS Mom's heart.

Mom: You need to focus on getting better.

Me: NOOOOOOO!

Mom: Calm down!

Me: I'M SEEING HER TONIGHT!

Mom: Stop yelling!

We'll talk more about this tonight.

This is why I didn't want to tell you.

I SLAM
the car door shut
as hard as I can.

Mom drives away.

I YELL,

I'M

SEEING

GRANDMA

TONIGHT!

Outpatient
Day 2
In the Cafeteria

I can't breathe
during breakfast.

Ruth: Jake, please eat your eggs.

I ignore her.

Ruth: Jake, you need to eat your eggs.

Me: Can I talk to Dr. Parker?

Ruth: After you eat your eggs!

The Voice: DON'T EAT THE EGGS!

Outpatient
Day 2
In Dr. Parker's Small and Tidy Office
Where I'm MAD at Mom and
FULL FROM EATING EGGS

....

I tell Dr. Parker
what Mom said.

I tell Dr. Parker
how Mom betrayed me.

I tell Dr. Parker
how Mom MUST TAKE ME TO
    GRANDMA.

Dr. Parker says,

Jake, take in a big, deep breath.

Count to three.

Let it out.

Take in a big, deep breath.

Count to three.

Let it out.

Again.

Dr. Parker helps me calm down.

She helps me slow down.

I think of what Grandma always says:
Slow and steady,
steady and slow,
that's the way to go.

Dr. Parker says,

I'll talk to your mom about visiting your
  grandma.

Is that OK?

I nod my head yes.

Thank you,
Dr. Parker!

Outpatient
Night 2
In Mom's Blue Car

....

Mom says
I can see Grandma
tomorrow night.

My heart
   sings
      and skips
         and worries
           A L L
              the
                  way
                    home.

Outpatient
Night 2
In My Bedroom
at My Parents' House

I pull a bright blue box
off the top shelf
in my closet.

Jacob Edward Stacey,
Age 3 to Age 7

is written on it
in Grandma's
loopy handwriting.

I open it.

Little Jake
looks up
at me.

He loves
pose-pose-posing

for Polaroids.

Funny poses,
sassy poses,
joyful poses.

So. Many. Poses.

Poses with
Grandma
next to a swimming pool.

Poses with
Grandma
at kindergarten graduation.

Full of life.
Smiling, shining, laughing, loving.

Will I ever love myself again?

Will anyone besides Grandma ever love me?

Outpatient
Day 3
Wednesday
Another Hard Day

....

Beep-Beep-Beep
goes the alarm clock
at 6:30 a.m.

Mom
drives
me to
Whispering Pines.

It takes
more than
an hour.

She sighs most of the way.

Mom says,

*Dr. Parker said it's OK for me to pick you
up at three to visit your grandma.*

Outpatient
Late Afternoon 3
In Grandma's ICU Room
at Palos Community Hospital

Machines
beep around
Grandma's bed.

Medicine
drips into
Grandma's veins.

Monitors
show Grandma's
vital signs.

Is that really Grandma?

beepbeepbeepbeepbeepbeepbeepb e e p
beepbeepbeepbeepbeepbeepbeepb e e p
beepbeepbeepbeepbeepbeepbeepb e e p
beepbeepbeepbeepbeepbeepbeepb e e p

Outpatient
Night 3
In Palos Community Hospital's Solarium

I can't breathe.

I think of what Dr. Parker said yesterday:

Take in a big, deep breath.

Count to three.

Let it out.

Take in a big, deep breath.

Count to three.

I repeat what Grandma always says:

Slow and steady,
steady and slow,
that's the way to go.

I can't catch my breath.

It feels like
a giant's
stomping
on my lungs.

The Voice says,

IT'S YOUR FAULT!

**IT'S
ALL
YOUR
FAULT!**

Take in a big, deep breath. Count to 3. Let
it out. Take in a big, deep breath. Count
to 3. Let it out. Take in a big, deep breath.
Count to 3. Let it out. Take in a big, deep
breath. Count to 3. Let it out. Take in a
big, deep breath. Count to 3. Let it out.
Take in a big, deep breath. Count to 3.
Let it out. Take in a big, deep breath.
Count to 3. Let it out. Take in a big, deep
breath. Count to 3. Let it out. Take in a
big, deep breath. Count to 3. Let it out.

Outpatient
Night 3
In Grandma's ICU Room
at Palos Community Hospital

The machines beep,
the medicine drips,
the lines go up and down.

I stare at Grandma,
wanting her to wake up,
waiting for her to wake up,
willing her to wake up.

I pull a photo
out of my pocket
and put it
next to her bed.

The photo of us
pose-pose-posing
next to a pool.

A photo from
better times,
calmer times,
happier times.

Before bullies
started throwing
verbal stones.

Before the Voice
started talking.

Before I
stopped eating.

Before Grandma
was hooked up to machines.

I whisper into Grandma's ear,

I love you to the moon and back.

I imagine she says,

I love you to the moon and back.

Now give your grandma a big SMOOCH
on the cheek!

Outpatient
Night 3
In My Bedroom
at My Parents' House

....

Dear Frieden,

Grandma needs your help.

Please.

She's sick.

It looks like a witch put a curse on her.

A curse of tubes.

A curse of machines.

A curse of IVs.

Please help her.

Please bless her.

Please protect her.

I need her.

Please.

Please.

Please.

Love,

Jake Stacey,
who loves talking to you
in Pondview Park
next to the library

Outpatient
Day 4
Art Therapy

....

Pedro's tie is covered in colorful hearts.

He says,

Today you'll draw your heart.

You can draw things you love inside your heart.

You can draw your feelings, your emotions, or maybe even a map of your heart.

There are heart templates on the yellow table and tons of art supplies on the green table.

Have fun exploring and creating art from and about your heart!

Draw my heart?

Really?

What does my heart look like?

Sad?

Stubborn?

Stuck?

Should I create a heart for Grandma?

A heart of our favorite things.

A heart of us.

I pick up a heart from the yellow table
and pull
pastels,
pens,
and colored pencils
out of my bag.

The art supplies Grandma gave me
for my fourteenth birthday.

Memories and moments
pour out of the pastels and pencils.

We're singing along to
Into the Woods in her red car.

We're reading
Goofy's Big Race in the living room.

We're eating extra-cheesy cheddar popcorn
while watching *Full House* and *Family
Matters* in the basement.

Memories and moments
that tattooed love on our hearts.

Love I once felt every day.

Pedro looks at my heart,
and says,
Wow! Well done, Jake!

*Did you make this beautiful heart for your
      grandma?*

I nod yes.

He says,

Are you going to give —

The Voice interrupts,

IT'S YOUR FAULT SHE'S SICK.

P O O F!

I
sink
back
into
myself.

Outpatient
Day 5
In Dr. Parker's Office

....

Dr. Parker and I
talk about how Grandma
loves movies and musicals.

She says,

*I think movies and musicals help you feel
closer to your grandma. As you know,
one of your treatment goals is to develop
healthy relationships with people your own
age. Movies and musicals could help you
feel closer to people your own age. When
you start high school in person, you could
join the Drama Club. You could help with
sets and costumes. You could even perform in plays and musicals one day.*

High school!

A new school.

Could I **REALLY**
perform?

Could I **STAND**
on a stage?

Could I **MAKE**
people laugh?

Could I **MAKE** people feel **HAPPY**
by performing,
by acting

ON   A   STAGE?

Outpatient
Night 5
Friday
In Room 468
at Palos Community Hospital

....

Machines still beep,
medicine still drips,
but Grandma's out of the ICU and
  awake.

Did Frieden help
reverse the curse?

Grandma says,

Get over here and give your grandma a
  BIG *smooch!*

I kiss Grandma's cheek.

She holds my hand and says,

I told your mom not to tell you I was sick.

She pauses.

You have enough to worry about.

You need to take care of my boy.

She pauses again.

I have more words for you, my dear grandbaby, but your grandma is too tired right now.

She closes her eyes.

I need to rest my eyes for a while.

I love you.

Grandma sleeps,

machines beep,

medicine drips . . .

I whisper in Grandma's ear,
I made this heart for you. I'll leave it on
the nightstand.

Outpatient
Night 5
Who Cares Where I Am?
Do You?

....

I talk to Emily Dickinson's photo.

Emily, home is hard.

Emily, eating is hard.

Emily, I can't stop
exercising
in the basement.

Emily, I hate myself.

Emily, I'm worried about Grandma.

Emily, it feels like
Grandma
and

I
are
both
lost in the woods.

Emily, my heart feels like
it's
bleeding;
like
it's
screaming
for someone
to come,
for someone
to rescue me.

The Voice says,

YOU ONLY NEED ME!

Do I?

Outpatient
Day 6
Saturday
In the Kitchen

....

Mom's tense.

She swears.

She sighs.

She says,

Jake, I can't walk on eggshells around you anymore.

You're moody.

You're miserable.

You're making everything harder than it needs to be.

Dr. Parker and Wanda told you to follow your meal plan during the weekend.

You refuse to help yourself.

Pancreatic cancer's destroying your grandma's body.

You're destroying your life by not eating.

STOP!

JUST STOP!

YOU NEED TO STOP THIS MADNESS!

LISTEN TO DR. PARKER AND RUTH!

WORK WITH HER ON WHY YOU HATE YOURSELF SO MUCH!

I'm sorry for yelling.
You need to take care of yourself.

You're loved.

People love you, Jacob!
Grandma loves you.
Your dad loves you.
I love you.

Please stop this madness.

Mom,
I

.

.

.
Mom,
I

.

.

.
Mom,
I

.

.

.
can't.

Mom repeats,

You can.

You can.

You can.

Outpatient
Night 6

....

The Voice
keeps me
awake
all night.

It's louder
than the hunger
again.

Outpatient
Day 7
Sunday
In the Kitchen

....

Mom's
YELLING.

YOU HAVE TO EAT!

YOU MUST EAT!

*I'M CALLING
DR. PARKER!*

Mom's on her
hands and knees,
begging me to eat.
CRYING.
BANGING
HARD, HARD, HARD
on the living room floor.

343

A Terrible, Horrible
Monday

I'm.
Locked.
Up.
Again.

ARRRRRRRRRRRRRRRRRRRR
RRRRRRRRRRRRRRRRRRRRRR
RRRRRRRRRRRRRRRRRRRRGG
GGGGGGGGGGGGGGGGGGGGG
GGGGGGGGGGGGGGGGGGGGG
GGGGGGGGGGGGGGGGGGGGG
GGGGGGGGGGGGGGGGGGGGG
HHHHHHHHHHHHHHHHHHH
HHHHHHHHHHHHHHHHHHH
HHHHHHHHHHHHHHHHHHH
HHHHHHHHHHHHHHHHHHH
HHHHHHHHHHHHHHHHHHH
HHHHHHHHHHHHHHHHHHH
HHHHHHHHHHHHHHHHHHH
HHHHHHHHHHHHHHHHHHH
HHHHHHHHHHHHHHHHHHH!

In Group Therapy

....

I'm not
playing an actor
in a play this time.

I'm not speaking in group.

Ruth can't make me.

I look around Ruth's circle.

Who are these other people?

I stopped listening.

I stopped keeping track
of other people's pain
        weeks ago.

I Don't Know What Day It Is
In Dr. Parker's Office

....

Dr. Parker: Are you ready to talk about why home was hard?

Me: No.

Dr. Parker: Are you ready to talk about why you're inpatient again?

Me: No.

We sit in solemn silence for

2 minutes,

4 minutes,

6 minutes.

Dr. Parker: Jake, please be kinder to yourself.

Me: I'm angry at myself . . .

Dr. Parker: Why?

Me: For being me.

For taking up space.

For existing.

For being a rotten grandson.

Dr. Parker: Jake, you didn't cause your grandma's cancer.

It isn't your fault.

You deserve —

I stop listening.
I feel tears
well up inside
my eyes.

Me: Can I go to the bathroom?

Dr. Parker: Yes.

I
bawl
and
bawl
and
bawl
in a bathroom stall.

All
alone
with a
pool
of tears.

Trapped in Whispering Pines

....

In the afternoon,
during free time,
Dr. Parker says,

Your mom and dad are here to see you.

They're waiting for you in the solarium.

I ignore her.

She says,

Jake, you should visit with your parents.

This is important.

I say,

I told
you

I don't
want
visitors.

Dr. Parker leaves.

I
won
this
battle.

Trapped in Whispering Pines
Continued

A few moments later,
Dr. Parker's back.

A folded sheet of yellow paper is in her
right hand. She sets it on the desk, in
front of me.

I recognize Mom's handwriting through
the paper.

Dr. Parker says,

*You don't want visitors right now, but
I need to share something with you.
It's important. How you receive this
information is entirely up to you.*

*Your mom wrote it on this piece of paper,
so you can read it yourself. Or, if you'd
like, I can tell you and we can talk about it.*

Whichever way you choose to receive the information is fine.

The only thing that isn't fine is for you not to know.

You can choose not to choose, of course. If you do, I'll leave the note here on your desk.

I pick up the piece of paper.

There are only six words written on it:

Your grandma died yesterday. I'm sorry.

I run like the wind
to the only window
facing Whispering Pines' parking lot.

I see Mom and Dad
driving away
in Grandma's red car.

Why did they drive her car?

I hear Grandma's voice in my head.

*Remember, one day you'll drive me
around town in my bright red car.
Remember, one day you'll drive me
around town in my bright red car.
Remember, one day you'll drive me
around town in my bright red car.*

Her voice sings inside my heart.

*Remember, take care of my boy.
Remember, take care of my boy.
Remember, take care of my boy.*

The VOICE chants,

**YOU STILL HAVE ME.
YOU STILL HAVE ME.
YOU STILL HAVE ME.**

I run
and
run
through
the
maze
of
hallways.

I slip and slide
into someone
holding a notebook.

It
F   L   I   E   S
through the air.

I say,

I'm sorry!

Kella says,

You look like you saw a phantom and it

wasn't happy.

Wait!
Kella's back?

Am I dreaming?

Kella says,

Are you OK?

Does this mean Grandma's
REALLY OK?

Will I wake up
ANY MOMENT NOW?

Is this all a
BIG NIGHTMARE?

I
run
and
run

back to room 165.

Wake up!

Wake up!

Wake up!

Wake up!

Wake up!

Not Dreaming
In Room 165

....

Later,
Pedro
knock-knock-knocks
on room 165's door.

He places a
big tray
on my desk.

Why's Pedro bringing me food?

Pedro says,

I talked to Dr. Parker.

I'm sorry for your loss, Jake.

You have to eat.

Even when you're sad.

*Even when you want to scream and shout
and throw your hands up in the air.*

Tonight you don't have to do it in the cafeteria.

You can eat in your room.

I look at his tie:
dragons eating donuts.

He says,

I'll sit with you.

We talk about Grandma.

We talk about Grandma's red car
and every movie and musical
Grandma and I love (loved?).

Pedro says,

*Jake, you're going to create beautiful
things throughout your life. I see it when
you create art. I know it. I see so many*

wonderful moments waiting for you.
Moments that will stay with you forever. I
hope you can see it yourself one day soon.

Please listen to Ruth and Dr. Parker.

Please work on getting better.

I think Grandma would like Pedro.

I think Grandma would trust Pedro.

Another Day in the Pines

....

Bruce hands me a
bright white envelope
and a piece of
yellow notebook paper.

Jake,
   I understand why you didn't want visitors yes-
terday afternoon. I understand why you didn't want
to talk on the phone last night. I was a lot like you
when I was fourteen. I hated talking on the phone. It
made my skin feel itchy. It made my heart race.
   We're more alike than you know.
   We feel a lot.
   We overreact a lot.
   We don't always know what we really want and
need. Our brains confuse us.
   Yesterday I found a letter your grandma was in
the middle of writing to you. I want you to have it.
Read it when you're ready. She loved you very much.
   I'm sorry for yelling at you. I should have been
more patient. This is hard on everyone, and I know
it's especially hard on you.

I love you!
Your mom

Grandma
wrote me
a letter?

Another Day in the Pines
Later

....

I stare out at nothing in the solarium.

Stare.

Stare.

Stare.

Someone **taps** on my shoulder.

It's Kella!

Kella's really back!

I didn't dream it.

Kella: Are you OK, Jake? You looked pretty upset a couple of days ago when you nearly knocked me down. I heard about your grandmother.

Words are written all over Kella's shoes
   in Sharpie:

   CADENCE and CONSONANCE

   IMPERFECT and IRONIC

   MAGIC and MOMENTS

If I didn't feel too sad to talk,
I'd ask why she's back in the Pines.

Kella: You don't have to say anything
right now. You look like you're in shock.
Breathe. Just breathe, Jake.

If I could breathe,
I'd tell her
how much I missed writing together in
   the solarium.

I do Dr. Parker's breathing exercises.

Take in a big, deep breath.

Count to three.

Let it out.

Take in a big, deep breath.

Count to three.

Kella: My brain feels pretty foggy right now, anyway. I feel like I'm walking through a field of clouds. I didn't think I'd ever come back to the Pines, but being out in the real world was hard. I stopped taking my medicine.

Me: I'm sorry.

If hugging weren't hard,
I'd hug her.

Kella: Don't be sorry. It isn't your fault.

Kella: I checked out the Broadway cast recording of *Into the Woods* from the Nichols Library.

Me: Really? You remembered to check it out?

Kella: I think I've listened to "Moments in the Woods" at least a hundred times. I get lost in Joanna Gleason's voice.

If it didn't feel like a giant was
crushing
my chest,
I'd share how Grandma and I will never sing that song together again.

Kella: I can see why you're obsessed with it. I'm gonna make you an epic mixtape as a thank-you one day. I'm gonna introduce you to my favorites.

If it didn't feel like a giant was
crushing
my bones,
I'd share that Grandma and I will never listen to our favorite show together again.

Kella: Your grandma's always with you.

Me: I'm sorry you're back in the Pines, but I missed you.

Kella: I missed seeing you, too. I'm gonna lie down. Maybe it will help my brain feel less foggy.

Kella waves and walks away.

Day 120

....

I sit in a
big blue chair
in the solarium.

I love
sinking
I N T O
its soft cushions.

I
feel
small.

Day 120
A Few Minutes Later

....

I hold
the
bright
white
envelope
up to the
light.

It glows.

I open it.

I unfold the paper.

I see
Grandma's
perfect,
loopy
cursive.

I smell
her
perfume.

It feels
like she's
beside me.

I take in a
deep breath.

I exhale,
sinking
into the
big blue
cushions.

I start reading.

Jake,

    I've been wanting to write you something ever since I heard about this burden you're carrying around with you. I haven't been capable of coming up with the right words.

    I wanted to be profound. You'll have to settle for Old Grandma and her elderly way with words.

    You're such a vital part of who I am, and what our family is all about. You're one of those HIGHLIGHTS. Life has a lot of downs and disappointments, but the faces of love ease hurt and give you the courage to fulfill your dreams.

    It sounds like a lecture.

    It's not.

    It's my life.

    I'm so privileged I was lucky enough to share your mom's labor and delivery. We weren't sure for a while if you were going to make it. Oh, how happy we were when you made your grand entrance. Laughing in between the tears of relief that you were in fact perfect. We were so happy bringing you home.

Jake, you can beat this burden if you try. I ask you, no I beg you, to get yourself better and go out into this beautiful world and enjoy life.

There's so much health and happiness ahead of you. It's your given right in this world to be healthy, and with health, comes happiness.

Jake, please give yourself permission to live your life to the fullest—you deserve it.

Just take it one day at a time, one step at a time. Set your mind on getting better.

These words are to remind you, my dear grandbaby, you are

I

am

what?

I'll never know.

After Reading Grandma's Unfinished Letter

....

I walk down
the maze of hallways
feeling like a zombie.

I think about
how Grandma
didn't finish,
will never finish,
writing the letter.

Day 121

....

I wake up thinking about Ms. Burns.

I miss
reading aloud
her mysteries.

I miss her
bright smile.

I miss her.

I hate talking on the phone,
like Mom shared in her letter.
It makes my skin feel itchy,
it makes my heart race,
but I want to hear Ms. Burns's voice.

I want to tell her about Grandma.

I wait for Bruce
at the nurses' station
for what feels like
a hundred years.

Bruce: Sorry for making you wait.
What's up?

Me: Can I call Ms. Burns at the Tinley
Terrace?

Bruce looks at me like I'm speaking a
secret language.

Me: Ms. Burns lives there. The Tinley
Terrace is a nursing home I volunteered
at every afternoon last year.

Bruce: I'll call Dr. Parker for permission.

I
wait
for

another
hundred
years.

Nurse Bruce: Dial seven-six on the
green phone.
Ms. Burns is waiting for you.

Me: Hello, Ms. Burns. Is that you?

Ms. Burns: Oh, Jake! Jake, how I've
missed your read-aloud voice. The
Tinley Terrace isn't the same without
you. How are you, my dear?

Tears
F
A
L
L

Day 122

....

My eyelids feel
as heavy as
an anvil.

Ruth leads
what she calls
mindfulness
exercises.

She turns off the lights.

Everyone lies on the floor.

I want to
sleep
and
sleep
and
sleep.

She tells us
to be present,
to breathe.

I think about how little I remember
from when Ms. Burns and I talked on
the phone.

It felt like I was underwater,
trying not to drown.

Your grandma loved you very much . . .

I miss your read-aloud voice . . .

Take care of your heart . . .

I think about what Kella said:

Your grandma's always with you.

Day 126

················

When Dr. Parker . . .

When Ruth . . .

When Bruce . . .

ask,

Jake, how are you feeling?

Do they really care?

Are they genuine?

How do you know
when someone
truly cares?

I think
everyone's trying

to trick me,
to confuse me.

How do you know when
to trust?

How do you know when
to believe?

Day 130

It's Thursday.

Thursday is

FACING

YOUR

FEAR

FOODS

DAY!

Wanda passes out a chart.

We write names
of foods
in boxes
labeled

Somewhat Fearful	Midsize Fearful	Extremely Fearful
		French fries

The Voice says,

WRITE DOWN EVERY FOOD YOU CAN THINK OF!!

I think of Grandma.

Of what she would want for me.

I say to the Voice,

I'M NOT GOING TO LIE.
LEAVE ME ALONE.

Day 130
Later

....

I love watching Kella
write-write-writing
in the solarium.

It looks like
light and music are

P O U R I N G

              out of her purple pen.

She looks
    S
        O
           O
              O
                  O
                      O
                          O
                              happy.

Kella puts down her purple pen
and says,

My aunt Karen's picking me up today.

Kella's leaving again?

I'm happy for her. Sad for me.

I say,

Keep taking your medicine.

Kella hugs me and hands me a note.

HI, JAKE,

IT'S ME, KELLA!

YOU MADE THE PINES MORE BEARABLE. I LOVE TALKING ABOUT BOOKS, MOVIES, AND MUSICALS WITH YOU. THANKS FOR ALWAYS LETTING ME BORROW YOUR ART SUPPLIES.

YOU'RE A GOOD FRIEND. I HOPE WE SEE EACH OTHER ONE DAY OUT IN THE REAL WORLD. MAYBE WE'LL GO TO A CONCERT OR MEET AT A MALL OR EXPLORE LIBRARIES AND BOOKSHOPS TOGETHER.

TAKE CARE OF YOURSELF.

EAT.

WRITE.

SING.

YOUR FRIEND,

KELLA ♥

Days 134 to 136

....

Dr. Parker loves assigning homework.

She says,

Make a list of five motivations to recover from anorexia nervosa.

After avoiding the assignment for a few days,

I write . . .

1. To get my driver's license.

2. To explore malls and bookshops and attend a concert with a best friend.

3. To go to college.

4. To work in a theater.

5. To travel.

Another Day
Another Therapy Session

················

Dr. Parker: Jake, thank you for sharing your goals. Can we talk about school?

Me: Why?

Dr. Parker: Your eating disorder started getting worse when you started middle school. Your mom told me you isolated yourself a lot.

Me: Can I write about it instead of talking about it?

Dr. Parker: OK. Will you share it with me?

Me: Maybe.

Day 146

....

Writing about middle school
feels like a dentist is
pulling out my teeth with pliers.

Here it goes.

Sixth grade had some good days.

Days when
the clothes I wore,
the show tunes I hummed,
the books I loved
didn't receive sneers and stares.

Days when
I walked down the hall
without someone
whispering

loser,

              wimp,

                            freak.

Seventh grade had more bad days than
    good.

Days when
I didn't want
to get out of bed.

Days when someone said
I walked the wrong way,
I talked the wrong way,
I WAS the wrong way.
Days when
I wished
I could

d
i
s
a
p
p
e
a
r

forever.

Eighth grade was awful
from the very first day.

I'm pretty sure Mom and Dad
heard me crying
myself to sleep
that night.

Most nights.

I'm pretty sure they
heard the
sobs
coming
out
of
my
bedroom.

In eighth grade,
we weren't just one big class anymore.

It seemed like somehow everyone
had snapped into these friend groups,
the places where they belonged,

except me.

There
was
no
room
in
any
group
for
me.

I was alone.

Stuck.

Every
single
day
I felt like I was on the outside,
looking in.

In eighth grade,
everyone also got

meaner,
more vicious.

Laughing,
staring,
whispering
as I walked by.

Notes in my locker.

Gum on my chair.

Tripping me in the hall.

I made up excuses
to avoid changing in the locker room
before gym class.

"My stomach hurts."

"I have a migraine."

"Can I go to the nurse?"

The locker room felt
like a torture chamber,
a place where I couldn't hide
inside baggy overalls
and big sweatshirts.

A place where
I felt trapped
with people who hated me,
with someone who snuck
back into the locker room one day
and peed all over my pants.

Peed inside my shoes.

Humiliated.

Forced to walk to the nurse's office in my
    gym shoes and shorts.

Forced to make up excuses to go home.

Ashamed.

I didn't tell anyone about my pee-soaked
  pants and shoes.

What would they do?

Teachers usually looked the other way,
anyway.

From then on,
I avoided the lunchroom.

I didn't eat.

I hid in the library.

       I hid in the art room.

             I hid in the bathroom.
I tried to disappear.

I repeated over and over
what Ryan (who used to be my neighbor)
and Kim (who used to sing silly songs on
  the bus with me)
and William (who came to my sixth
  birthday party at McDonald's)

whispered as I passed them in the hall:

"You're a nobody!"

"What a loser!"

"Why do you even exist?"

Words that whirled around
inside my head
like a dust devil.

I believed them.

I told myself I didn't deserve to live.

The Voice helped
drown out the sounds
of everyone else.

I had
too much
time alone
with the Voice.

I welcomed it in.

I told it to take a seat.

It calmed me
at first.

It made me
feel strong.

It made me
feel in control.

It
felt
like
what
I
wanted
most:
a
best
friend.

It
said
I would
be
the
best
at
not
eating.

It
said
I
didn't
need
food.

I listened.

I learned.

I lied to everyone.

I
gave
in
to
my
eating
disorder.

It
controlled
me
when
I thought
I controlled
it.

Day 150

....

Dr. Parker: Did you write about school?

Me: Yes.

Dr. Parker: Will you share it with me?

Me: OK.

I can feel
she's surprised.

I think of Grandma and Ms. Burns
as I read it aloud.

I cry.

She hands me a tissue.

I cry harder.

She tells me to
let it
O U T.

It feels freeing to share.
It feels good to admit
out loud for the first time
how lonely and lost
I felt as people made fun of me
day after day,
as they told me how much they hated me
for being me.
It feels good to let it

O   U   T.

Day 162

I keep a list of expressions Ruth often
  repeats.

I never know if they're her original
  thoughts

OR

if she borrowed them.

*Jake, life can only be lived forward but
  understood backward.*

Jake, legalize all foods.

*Jake, losing weight is one thing, losing per-
  spective is another.*

Jake, do you think I was born yesterday?

I ask
why she always
uses my name.

*Jake, your name can be music to your
ears.*

Day 166

....

Dr. Parker asks
why I rarely talk
about my dad.

You talk about your grandma.

You talk about your mom.

Why not your dad?

I don't know
what to say.

Which words
describe our
relationship?

Complicated?

Strained?

Tense?

Memories from
second or third grade
flood my mind.

Dad's walking
me to school.

There I am,
walking way
ahead of him.

There's an
embarrassed,
angry
eight-year-old.

Embarrassed by the
grease on Dad's hands,
the dirt on his clothes
from excavating foundations
and digging ditches.

404

There's Jake,
hurting Dad's
feelings,
lashing out.

Angry
he smelled like an ashtray.

Angry
we had nothing to talk about.

Angry
I wasn't tougher,
more like him
and less like me.

A N G R Y

FOR

ALWAYS

BEING

SO SENSITIVE!

Day 173

....

Dr. Parker says,

Jake, your mom and I talked yesterday.
I told her it's time for you to receive a day
pass. One day next week, you'll leave here
in the morning and return in the evening.
Your mom will plan the day, including
eating at a restaurant.

Does this sound OK to you?

I say,

I'll try.

The Voice says,

YOU WON'T EAT!

Day 178
A Day Pass
Act 1

I meet Mom in
Whispering Pines' lobby
at 11:45 a.m.

She hugs me.

I freeze like ice.

She signs me out.

I follow her like a prisoner.

As we head to
an unknown destination,
I hear Grandma's voice say,

You can do this, Jake!

Be nice!

You can do this, Jake!

Cooperate!

Jake, you can do this!

I hear Grandma's soothing voice,
bouncing around inside my head,
like a song,
an earworm
on repeat.

Y O U

C A N

D O

T H I S,

J A K E !

Mom parks
the car
in a garage
across the street from
the Chicago Theatre.

Are
we
seeing
a
show?

An usher
leads us to the
fourth row,
    center.

We sit in chairs
the brightest
shade of red.

Red,
the color of Grandma.

Did Grandma know this
shade of red exists?

An usher hands me a program.

Beauty and the Beast!

I read every performer's bio.

The lights dim.

        My heart flutters.

The Overture starts.

        My heart flies.

The Prologue starts.

        I hear

clarinets,   trumpets,   a piano,
      violins,   a cello.

So many
enchanting
sounds.

A deep voice

F I L L S

the theater.

As the show unfolds,

I absorb
    every note,
        every lyric,
            every colorful set,
                every costume
                change.
Like Belle,
am I
strange
but
special?

Do I want
much more than
what this
eating disorder
gives me?

I want
adventure.

I
want
so
much
more.

I can't stop smiling
in the lobby
during intermission.

Mom: Watching you watch *Beauty and the Beast* made my heart happy. I could feel the energy from the stage bouncing back and forth between you and Belle.

It sounds like she's talking about
    someone else.

Did I look the way Kella does
when lyrics are flowing
out of her purple pen?

Mom: You looked so happy. Truly happy.

I hug her,
even though
hugging is hard.

Me: I wish Grandma were here with us.

She tears up.

Mom: So do I! You and your grandma
shared such a special bond. You
understood each other. I felt jealous
sometimes. I'm sorry I haven't always
been the mom you needed. I know I
haven't always been the mom you wanted.
I hope you know I love you very much.

Me: I love you, Mom.

The lobby lights flicker
off and on,
        off and on,
                off and on.

A deep voice announces,

This afternoon's performance of Beauty
and the Beast *will resume in two minutes.*

Please return to your seats.

A Day Pass
Act 2

....

The house lights dim.

I hear a piccolo
followed by
an oboe
and a clarinet.

They fill my heart with light.

I want
to live
inside the instruments' sounds.

I want
to live
inside Belle's library.

I want
to live
inside

this
happy
moment
forever.

I want
to live
on a
stage.

The Voice shouts
　　LOUDLY
during "The Mob Song,"
a scene where
angry villagers
storm Beast's castle.

It says,

YOU DON'T DESERVE HAPPINESS!

MOM'S TAKING YOU TO A RESTAURANT!

YOU BETTER NOT EAT!

I hush it.

I tell it to leave me alone.

I beg the Voice to please
let me enjoy
this moment,
this experience,
this pure joy.

A Day Pass
Act 3

....

At dinner,
Mom catches me
hiding bits of
butter and beef
inside the napkin
on my lap.

She makes me
order
a new
serving.

I refuse
to
eat
it.

The Voice whispers,

KEEP RESISTING!

I refuse to talk.

I cross my arms.

I curl inside myself.

Mom says,

Please eat.

We were having such a nice day.

We loved Beauty and the Beast.

We were so happy during it.

I pick up
my plate.

Mom says,

Put it down now.

You wouldn't.

Put it down now.

Put it down right this second, Jake.

She reaches for the plate.

The Voice shouts,

DO IT!

I **hurl** it
as hard
as I can

ACROSS   THE   RESTAURANT

I   TOSS   IT

LIKE

A

FRISBEE.

Beef,

beans,

broccoli,

bread,

and

butter

FLY

FREE.

The Voice **CHEERS!**

The Car Ride
Back to
Whispering Pines

....

is silent.

A BLAH Day

....

Dr. Parker says,

*I talked to your mom. She told me you had
a hard time yesterday.*

I cross my arms.

*Maybe it will help you to know that
this kind of thing tends to happen, has
happened with other patients.*

I glare at her.

*That's kind of why we give the passes in
the first place. The idea is that it's better
to struggle when you can come back here
and we can process it, make sense of it
together, so that it's less likely to happen
when you go home for good.*

Let's talk about —

I interrupt her.

I say,

I need a break
from you.

I'm tired of talking
about my feelings.

I'm tired of you
bringing up
underlying issues.

I'm tired
of when you
tap-tap-tap
YOUR STUPID PEN.

I'm tired
of you.

I stand up.

Dr. Parker says,

Jake, please stay. Our time isn't up yet.

I walk to the door.

I turn the knob.

I turn around and say,

Do you want to know how I feel, Dr. Parker?

I'M BLISSFUL!

EVERYTHING'S PERFECT!

EVERYTHING'S GREAT!

I run down the long maze of hallways.

Tears
fall
and
fall
as
I

sit
on
the
floor
in
room
165.

It's just
me and the Voice,
the vicious Voice and me,
alone

       together

            in
            this
            depressing
            place.

Another Blah Day

....

Why
am
I
so
mean?

Why
am
I
so
cruel?

Why
can't
I
pull
myself
together?

Why
does
it
feel
like
there's
an
infected
cavity
inside
my
mind?

Why
can't
I
silence
the
Voice?

I Don't Care
What Day It Is!

....

I've refused
everything
for five days.

Refused to write.

Refused to attend sessions with Dr. Parker.

Refused group therapy.

Refused most meals.

Refused to talk.

Refused

IT ALL!

Another Day

···············

Dr. Parker sits
on a stiff chair
next to my bed.

She's
tap-tap-tapping
her pen again.

I won't
make
eye contact.

She says,

Jake, you've lost too much weight.

The Voice says,

GOOD!

GREAT!

THE BEST NEWS OF THE CENTURY!

She says,

If you lose more weight, you'll receive a feeding tube.

The tube will put calories directly into your stomach.

Dr. Parker's lying.

She wouldn't do that.

Yet Another Day
Another Weigh-In

....

I hear Wanda's high heels
clack-clack-clacking
toward room 165.

She wheels a scale into the room.

Clunk

Tick

Tick

Tick

go the sliding weights on the scale.

Day 186

....

Dr. Parker says,

Nurse Bruce will meet you in a few minutes.

She reminds me
this was the plan
if I lost more weight.

Bruce
walks me to
an examining room.

He preps
everything:

tube,
tape,

cup,
straw,

433

bottles
filled
with
tons
of
calories,

and
things
I cannot
identify.

A doctor in green scrubs
enters the room.

She says,

I'm Dr. Khan. I'm going —

Get away from me.

I kick.

I scream.

I cover my nose.

They leave.

Did I really win this battle?

Fifteen Minutes Later

Dr. Parker returns.

She says,

You've refused everything.

This is where we are.

I told you this was the plan.

Dr. Khan will be back in fifteen minutes.

Pull yourself together.

Ten Minutes Later

....

Frieden,
I wish
I were
stronger.

Frieden,
are you here?

Frieden,
I need your help.

The Saga Continues
Five Minutes Later

....

I close
my eyes.

I bite
my lip.

I hold
Bruce's hand
as Dr. Khan
inserts a
thin tube
through my
right nostril.

She tells me to
drink water
through
a straw
as the tube
makes its way to
my stomach.

438

It feels like
my head's going to
EXPLODE.

She tapes the tube to my face.

I lie on
my back
as Bruce
pours a pinkish liquid
into a clear bag.

It

drips,

drips,

drips

directly
into my
stomach.

The Voice says,

Pull out the —

I cut it off.

But I don't want
to mess up
                again.

I'm tired of
messing up
                again
                        and
                                again.

Day 3
with the Tube

Today's
Ruth's turn to sit on
the stiff chair
next to my bed.

She talks about
revisiting goals
I wrote
a million years ago.

I wish the Voice would let me say,

I miss group therapy.
I miss art therapy.
I'm bloated.
I'm lonely.

Instead,

I ignore her.

Day 7
with the Tube

....

Dr. Khan
removes
the
tube.

I
never,
never,
never,
never
want
a
tube
again.

Day 194

....

Dr. Parker says,

*Jake, I'm happy we're meeting in my office
    again.*

We discuss
feelings,
fears,
and
failures.

We discuss
how I
thought the
Voice was my friend.

We discuss
how it
comforted me at first,
how it helped me deal

with how lonely and strange
I felt at school.

Dr. Parker says,

I know this is difficult.

*It's time to really talk back to your eating
    disorder.*

There are many reasons to get better.

You can get better to help others.

You can get better to travel.

You can get better to join a drama club.

You can get better to go to college.

*You can get better to sing show tunes
from* Into the Woods *and* Beauty and the
Beast *at the top of your voice.*

But, Jake, get better for yourself.

Do it for you.

I see your kind, compassionate heart.

I see you.

You have a full life to live and lead.

But you must do the work.

I say,

I wish
I could eat
without feeling
guilty,
unworthy.

Dr. Parker says,

Give yourself permission.

I say,

I'm sorry for
yelling at you.
I'm sorry for
being such a jerk.

I'll set
my mind
on getting
better.

I'll do it
for Grandma.

I'll do it
to visit Broadway one day.

I'll do it for me.

I really will.

As I close
Dr. Parker's door,
the Voice SCREAMS,

THIS MEANS YOU'LL —

I SCREAM back
louder
than
it.

**LEAVE
ME
ALONE!**

**LEAVE
ME
ALONE!**

**LEAVE
ME
ALONE!**

Day 194
Later
In the Cafeteria

....

During dinner,
I picture Frieden
on her pedestal
in the park.

I imagine
she hears:

ducks quacking,

      baseballs cracking,

            babies crying.

As I eat corn casserole,
I talk to her in my mind.

Frieden,
please
help

me
silence
the
voice.

Frieden,
please
help
me
make
Grandma
proud.

Frieden,
please
help
me
help
myself.

Day 195

....

Frieden,
can
you
really
hear
me?

You
visited
me
in
a
dream
last
night.

You
and
your
four

cherubs
calmed
and
comforted
me.

You

R
    E
       A
          C
             H
                E
                    D

out
your
right
hand,
offering
a
blessing.

You
told
me
to
talk
back
to
the
voice.

You
encouraged
me
to
write
a
letter
to
Grandma.

You
gave
me
strength.

Day 203

....

I rip a
piece of paper
out of my notebook.

Dear Grandma,

Sorry it took so long to write back. I wish I knew what you were going to write next in your letter. I think about it every day.

You are . . .

I am what?

If you knew that I haven't gone to school in a long time, I think you would write that . . .

You are
ASHAMED OF ME.

You are
DISAPPOINTED IN ME.

You are
SICK OF ME ACTING LIKE A BRAT.

You are
SAD I'M NOT TAKING CARE OF YOUR BOY.

Everything's hard. It feels like there's always an angel and a devil sitting on my shoulders.

The devil is a voice, telling me not to eat, to restrict. That I don't deserve food. That I'm unworthy of living. That the feelings inside me are wrong.

The angel says, please help yourself.

The devil usually wins.

Dr. Parker always says,

You need to feed your brain.

I want to work on this burden. I want to silence the voice.
I'm trying. I really am. I want to take care of your boy.

Slow and steady,

steady and slow,

that's the way to go.

It will be different this time, right?

I hope.

Love,

Jake

P.S. Mom and I saw the musical Beauty and the
Beast in Chicago.

Mom and I wished you had been there with us. You
would have loved it. The red seats. The performers. The
songs. The costumes. The story.

I think about it every day. It made my heart happy.

Maybe I'll see Into the Woods on Broadway one day.
Wouldn't that be amazing? Wow!

455

Day 211

....

Dr. Parker
nods
as I share
how much I love
Emily Dickinson's poetry.

A picture of Kella
write-write-writing away
in the solarium
pops into my mind.

Dr. Parker: Are you OK? It looked like
you left the room for a moment.

Me: Can you add Kella's name to my
approved visitors list?

Dr. Parker: Why?

Me: She reminds me of Emily Dickinson when she writes songs in her notebook. She's nice to me. I think she understands me. I think we understand each other.

Dr. Parker
looks surprised.

For the first time,
it almost looks like
she's without words.

Dr. Parker: It's a bit of an unusual request, but I understand why you're asking. And it's in keeping with one of your treatment goals of developing friendships with people your own age. I'm glad you're taking ownership of your treatment. If Kella's an important person in your life now, that's rationale for seeing if I can add her name to your visitors list. I'll look into it. I'll get back to you soon.

Me: Thank you, Dr. Parker!

Dr. Parker: I'm happy you're being assertive in a more positive way.

July 1997

Dear Grandma,

It's me again. I miss you. Wanda serves fear foods from our charts on Thursdays. It's getting easier. I'm cooperating, I'm doing the work. I'm addressing "underlying issues." (Dr. Parker's phrase.)

I'm not ready to eat French fries. I'm working toward it. I'm trying. I'm doing it for you, but I'm also doing it for me.

Your boy,

Jake

P.S. Mom and Dad visited last week.

They surprised me with the original Broadway cast recording of Rent and my portable CD player. Dr. Parker approved both.

Whoa! I nearly fell over. It's an intense rock musical. Idina Menzel's big voice makes my soul SING and SOAR. It takes place in New York City. A city we wanted to visit together.

Maybe I'll still visit NYC one day. I'm listening to it on repeat.

I hear,

I see,

I discover

things about myself.

I think theater is part of who I am.

You would have loved it. You would have embraced it.

P.P.S. I love you!

Slow and steady,

steady and slow,

that's the way to go.

P.P.P.S.

Writing letters to you soothes my heart, my soul, my mind.

P.P.P.P.S.

I'm SUPER EXCITED! Dr. Parker said Kella can visit in a few weeks. I think you'd like her. We met at

Whispering Pines. She's a sophomore at Naperville Central High School. She loves poetry and musicals like we do.

Like you did.

Writing about you in the past tense feels like a giant's crushing my toes, crushing my bones, crushing me.

Like Kella said to me one day in the middle of a maze of hallways,

Your grandma's always with you.

Kella's right.

I can feel you with me.
Always.

Day 237

....

Mom brings
a big bag of my books
to Whispering Pines.

I spot my collection of
Emily
Dickinson's
poems.

I read aloud poem 254:

Hope is the thing with feathers
That perches in the soul,
And sings the tune without the words,
And never stops at all,

And sweetest in the gale is heard;
And sore must be the storm
That could abash the little bird
That kept so many warm.

I've heard it in the chillest land,
And on the strangest sea;
Yet, never, in extremity,
It asked a crumb of me.

It
perches
in my
soul.

I find a note written to Frieden,
who I pretended was my real-life best
    friend,
tucked inside it . . .

Sunday, August 28, 1994

Hi, Frieden,

How are you?
How are your cherubs????
I hope you're all doing well.
Guess what?
I got out of gym class for one week.
NO GYM CLASS!
I'M SO HAPPY!
HOORAY!

Your best friend,
Jake

Wow!

Look how lonely Jake feels.
Look how desperately
he needs,
wants
friends.

Why do I feel
protective of
   him?

I want to help
eleven-year-old me.

464

Day 239

....

I show Dr. Parker
my letter to Frieden.

I tell her
how I felt
after reading it.

She says,

Jake, he's you.

You're Jake.

*Sometimes you talk about your
experiences from such a distance.*

You can change your future.

*Keep talking back to what you refer to as
the voice inside your head.*

*I see how hard you've been working
toward recovery.*

465

Day 239
Later

....

Dr. Parker's right.

I'm doing the work.

I'm
cooperating
less
and
less
with
the voice.

I'm
cooperating
more
and
more
with
Ruth,
Bruce,

466

Wanda,
and
Dr. Parker.

I'm telling the voice to
be quiet.

I'm telling the voice to
leave me alone.

I'm doing it for
Grandma.

I'm doing it for
Frieden.
I'm doing it for

ME.

Day 243

....

Dr. Parker says,

I talked to your mom and dad yesterday.
We all agree you're ready for another
day pass. You'll get a redo from what
happened after Beauty and the Beast.
You're in a better position to handle it.

Do you agree?

I say,

Yes, I'm ready.

Dr. Parker says,

Good! Your dad will pick you up tomorrow
  afternoon.
We believe in you.

I can do it.
Can't I?

Day 244
Scene 1

....

Dad's silver pickup truck
usually smells like a wet ashtray.

Not today.

Dad says,

You look healthier, Jake.

The voice says,

HE MEANS YOU LOOK —

Count to three.

Breathe in.

Don't listen to the voice.
       Don't listen to the voice.
              Don't listen to the voice.
Count to three.

Breathe out.

You can do this.
               You can do this.
                              You can do this.
He says,

Let's visit a bookshop and then we'll eat lunch at a diner in Chicago.

A bookshop?

Dad doesn't read books.

In Chicago?

Dad thinks there's "too much traffic in the city."

Dad says,

Let's do something you love.
Let's have a good day.

I can do this.   I can do this.

Three black-and-white banners
　flap flap flap
　in the wind.

I pretend they're chanting,

Welcome!　　Welcome!　　Welcome!

Beneath the banners,

light illuminates books
lined up in windows.

I pretend they're shouting,

Pick me!   Pick me!   Pick me!   Pick me!

Pick me!
                    No, pick me!

Dad says,

Come on! Let's go inside!

Day 244
Scene 3

It feels like stepping inside
a different world,
a calmer place,
a kinder place.

It smells like hope.

Dad says,

*I'll meet you in the front of the store in
twenty minutes.*

I wander and roam
up and down
aisles filled with
comic books,
calendars,
magazines,
science fiction.

I pick up a copy of Lois Lowry's *The
    Giver,*
hug it tight to my chest like the blanket
Grandma crocheted for me when I was
    two.

I pause in front of
a giant picture book wall.

There's a bear and a hare,
a dog named Gloria,
a tall angel . . .

I hear Grandma's voice in my heart
    saying,
You're never too old to read picture books.

A full smile slips out.

I don't pull it back inside.

Day 244
Scene 4

....

I'm a little lost inside my head,
thinking about Grandma and
how I want to live inside this bookshop
  forever,
when I bump into someone
with a boy-band bob haircut
holding *The Poems of Emily Dickinson.*

Before I can stop myself,
I say,

I'm Nobody! Who are you?
Are you — Nobody — too?

He says,

There is no Frigate like a Book
To take us Lands away,
Nor any Coursers like a Page
Of prancing Poetry —

I say,

Hope is the thing with feathers
That perches in the soul

His dimples appear.

He says,

I'm impressed.

A laugh slips out.

Sometimes I forget
how nice it
feels to laugh.

I say,

I'm Jake.

Sorry for bumping into you.

He says,

477

I'm Mike.

I'm glad you did. This was my first time reciting poetry in the middle of Unabridged Books.

I say,

I thought I was the only fourteen-year-old who recites Emily Dickinson's poems.

He says,

You're not the only one. Trust me.

I'm president of the Poetry Club at my high school.

We're memorizing Emily Dickinson's poems this month.

I hear Dad calling for me.

Jake, where are you?

Jake!

Jake!

I say,

I have to go.

My dad's waiting for me.

It was fun reciting Emily's poetry with you.

He says,

> *To see the Summer Sky*
> *Is Poetry, though never in a Book it lie —*
> *True Poems flee —*

I wave
goodbye.

Day 244
As Dad and I Walk to Lunch

....

Did that really just happen?

Did I imagine it?

Was he a bookshop ghost?

A Poetry Club?

Are there really people who love reciting poetry like Mike and me?

Could I join a poetry club when I start high school in person?

Day 244
Scene 5

....

A pink-and-blue neon sign flashes

MELROSE
DINER

PANCAKE
SPECIALTIES

OPEN
24 HRS

The host hands us menus
as thick as bibles.

A book filled with
omelets and scramblers,
pancakes and waffles,
Benedicts and burgers,
soups and sandwiches.

The voice wakes up.

Count to three.

Breathe in.

You're having a good day.
        Food keeps you alive.
                You can have a happy life.

Count to three.

Breathe out.

Day 244
Scene 6

················

As I eat eggs Benedict and fresh fruit,
Dad asks about *The Giver.*

He listens as I go on and on
about Jonas and the Committee of Elders
  and the Receiver of Memory.

Dad asks about *The Complete Works of*
  Emily Dickinson.

He's interested as I go on and on
about feathers and hope and birds and
  poems fleeing.

I ask him about excavating.

He lights up like a Christmas tree.
He talks about

foundations and ditches and engines
the way I feel about books and musicals
   and poetry.

Maybe we're not so different.

Day 244
Scene 7

....

As we drive by Unabridged Books,
I say *thank you* in my mind.

I imagine myself living
near this neighborhood
one day,

walking up the steps of a brownstone
I call home,

visiting bookshops every day,

eating in diners without fear with future
friends,

reciting Emily's poems to
strangers.

Day 244
Scene 8

....

Dad says,

Jake, wake up!

Wake up, Jake!

We're back at Whispering Pines.

Was today a dream?

I hug Dad in Whispering Pines' lobby
and say,

Today was a perfect day, Dad!

Hugging isn't as hard
as it used to be.

Day 246

....

I tell Dr. Parker about reciting poetry
at Unabridged Books and eating eggs
Benedict in a fun diner.

She says,

Congratulations on a successful day pass.

*It sounds like you're ready to revisit your
goals.*

I pull out a purple pen.

I add a sixth goal.

1. To get my driver's license.
2. To explore malls and bookshops
   and attend a concert with a best
   friend.
3. To go to college.

487

4. To work in a theater.

5. To travel.

6. To join a poetry club.

Day 251
Visiting Day

....

I'm reading Shel Silverstein's
Where the Sidewalk Ends
in the solarium
when someone taps on my shoulder.

I know who it is right away!

K	K	K
E	E	E
L	L	L
L	L	L
A	A	A

Kella's really here in the Pines.

Not as a patient
but as a visitor this time.

We hug.

The voice says,

SHE —

Count to three.

Breathe in.

Don't listen to the voice.
      Don't listen to the voice.
            Don't listen to the voice.

Breathe out.

Kella talks about
the lyrics she's writing.

Songs about her depression,
      about going into the Pines,
            about finding her way out.

She talks about
the clubs she joined.

Glee Club,
      Drama Club,
            Comics Club.

490

I tell her about
Unabridged Books.

About the walls and walls
filled with BOOKS.

About bumping into Mike
in the Poetry section.

About reciting
Emily Dickinson's poems together.

About how he's president of
the Poetry Club.

She says,

WoWSERS! You're beaming!

I feel my ears turning red.

She says,

You can join the Poetry Club at your high school. And if they don't have one, you'll start one. I can't wait for you to get out of the Pines.

Kella picks up
Shel Silverstein's
Where the Sidewalk Ends.

The pages are
dog-eared,
torn,
tattered,
stained,
and
loved.

The spine is
brittle,
broken,
barely
hanging on,
and
loved.

Most fourteen-year-olds
don't carry around
a book they loved
in the second grade.

The poems
comfort me.

Kella doesn't find it strange.

She reads aloud

"Sarah Cynthia Sylvia Stout Would Not
Take the Garbage Out"

in the most
amazing,
delightful
way.

I ask,

How did you learn to read it aloud like
    that?

She says,

From Tori Amos, the greatest musician of all time.

She recorded herself performing the poem.

It's BRILLIANT!

I'll lend you Tori's albums.

I think you'll love her.

I recite
"The Sitter"
from memory.

Kella asks,

When did you memorize it?

I say,

When I "forced"
my imaginary students to
memorize it.

She laughs.

I laugh.

Laughter

FILLS

and

FLOODS

the

room

with

light.

Day 251
Part 2

....

Kella's aunt Karen
picked her up
a few minutes ago.

I cannot stop smiling,
thinking about how
we read aloud
— performed really —
Shel's poems.

I open *Where the Sidewalk Ends.*

I take in
what Grandma
wrote inside it.

I love her handwriting.

This Book Belongs to Jake E. Stacey

June 6, 1989

This marvelous collection of poetry was given to Jake because he worked so hard at school & received such good grades.

Hugs and kisses,

Grandma

P.S. Take care of my boy.
P.P.S. I love you to the moon and back.

Day 254

....

Pedro talks about
mindfulness,
emotional waves,
how to put
emotions into
an imaginary box
and set it on a shelf.

Pedro talks about
how making art
can help us
express pain,
tell stories,
heal.

I **LOVE**
art therapy now.

I **LOVE**
putting paint
on paper,

smearing all the
colors
TOGETHER.

I **LOVE**
noticing Pedro's fun ties.

Today's tie?

Jumbo smiley faces.

I **LOVE**
searching through
magazines,
cutting out
photos and drawings
to create colorful collages.

I **LOVE**
drawing what
fear and guilt,
hope and happiness
look like to me.

I **LOVE**
how Pedro
plays music
as we
create papier-mâché masks.

I **LOVE**
how Pedro
encourages expressing
emotions through art,
how he
listens,
how he
helps me
feel **safe**.

I **LOVE**
art therapy.

Day 255

I'm in the solarium,
watching sunlight shine in
through every window.

Watching motes of
   dust d a n c e

A   C   R   O   S   S
         the
         room.

It's where I
read.

It's where I
write.

It's where I
reflect.

It's where I
think about Grandma.

It's where I
mentally replay
every therapy session,
judging,
digesting,
dissecting,
contemplating
everything I said,
everything I shared.

It's where I organize
thoughts . . .

It's where I organize
details . . .

It's where I
file away
everything.

Day 264

....

Bruce
knock-knock-knocks
on room 165's door.

He says,
Kella left a note and a mixtape for you
at the front desk yesterday. Dr. Parker
approved that you can have them.

My heart cheers.

HI, JAKE,

I WAS GOING TO WAIT UNTIL THE NEXT TIME WE SAW
EACH OTHER TO GIVE YOU THIS MIXTAPE, BUT I WAS
AT THE PINES FOR A MEETING WITH MY THERAPIST
TODAY.

I HOPE DR. PARKER LETS YOU HAVE IT.
I CALL THE MIXTAPE "HEALING TUNES."
IT INCLUDES SONGS AND ARTISTS I THINK
YOU'LL LOVE—LIKE SARAH MCLACHLAN'S "I WILL
REMEMBER YOU," TINA TURNER'S "THE BEST,"
ALANIS MORISSETTE'S "PERFECT," AND TRACY
CHAPMAN'S "THE PROMISE."

I HOPE YOU LIKE IT.

YOUR FRIEND,

KELLA ♥

Night 264

It's 11:11 p.m.

Kella's
mixtape
plays
on
repeat.

I take in
each
angelic
voice.

I analyze
every note,
each lyric.

Their
voices
quiet

and
calm
the
negative
voice
inside
my
head.

The
music
helps
me
think.

It
feels
like
every
artist
understands
me.

Their
songs
help
me
imagine
a life
outside
Whispering
Pines.

Their
voices
help
me
imagine

a better life,
        a brighter life,
                a healthier life.

....

Frieden,
Kella's mixtape
comforts me
like you do when
I
see
your
arm

REACHING OUT

to

me.

Day 270

....

Pedro thinks
about our
hearts a lot.

And I think
about his
fun ties a lot.

Colorful stacked figures
dance down his tie today.

Pedro says,

*Marsha, Donna, Danielle, and Jake, you
can make whatever you'd like today.*

*There are tons of art supplies on the yellow
and green tables.*

Ask yourself this question:

What does my heart need *to create today?*

I study
everything
on the yellow table.

I think about
how Grandma
always said,
Jake, take it all in.

I pick out
paper,
shapes,
tinsel,
tiny scraps,
anything
and
everything
that speaks
to my heart.

I **CREATE**
a colorful collage
inspired by

Into the Woods,

Beauty and the Beast,

Unabridged Books,

Tori Amos.

I show it to Pedro.

He says,

Jake, you created art from the heart.

I say,

Thanks for believing in me when I didn't
    believe in myself!

Day 278

....

We're sitting in a circle,
a circle of trust.

Ruth asks,

What's your favorite word?

Marsha's favorite word is *loquacious.*

She loves how it

R
    O
       L
          L
            S

off her tongue.

Donna thinks *incandescent*
has a musical,
lyrical quality.

Danielle thinks *serendipitous* sounds
  hopeful.

Bombastic is Barb's favorite word.

She says
each syllable
s l o w l y.

bom   bas   tic

As everyone shares,
I think about Ms. Wozny.

She wrote
what she called
WOW words
on the chalkboard
every day.

Ms. Wozny said,

A WOW word makes you feel something.
A WOW word makes you stop and think.

I wrote her WOW words
inside a purple notebook.

I carried the notebook
everywhere.

I studied the definitions,
always looking for
ways to slip
the perfect word
into a conversation.

Clangorous | Adjective

Definition: *A loud and continuous sound.*

Example:
The clangorous voice convinced me
I liked hunger pains.

Fastidious | Adjective

Definition: *Attentive to detail.*

Example:
I'm a fastidious eater.

Or so I thought.

Salubrious | Adjective

Definition: *Healthy.*

Example:
I thought restricting was a salubrious
  behavior.

Wanderlust | Noun

Meaning: *A want and need to travel.*

Example:
I have an intense case of wanderlust.

It started the day
I learned that
perfect word.

I carry
wanderlust,
the word,
the feeling,
everywhere
with me.

I collect
maps,
guides,
brochures
about
states
FAR,
FAR,
FAR
away
from
here.

Just look
inside
my desk;
the second drawer on the   **RIGHT.**

516

You'll see
places I
dream about.

Places I yearn
to visit.

Places I want
to live.

I'm ready
to listen to
Dr. Parker.

I'm tired of
insalubrious
behaviors.

I'm tired of
anorexia nervosa
defining me,
controlling every
thought and action.

Can I be as
fastidious
about recovery
as I was about
being sick?

Ruth says,

Jake, do you have a favorite word?

I say,

My favorite word is *wanderlust.*

I love how it sounds.

I want to say it
ALL the time.

I love how it feels as
I write each letter:
W A N D E R L U S T

Seven consonants,
three vowels.

I love how it looks
in my mind
as I write it down.

It makes me feel
hopeful
and
happy.

It makes me
feel emotions
I'm not sure
how to describe.

I walk over to the
whiteboard,
pick up a
purple marker,
and write . . .

I think it's part of who I am.

Day 302

....

Dr. Parker: Jake, over the past three months, you've been more open and honest during our meetings and during group-therapy sessions. You're addressing the hurt and confusion. You're working through the issues. You're doing the work to get better, and the medications are helping you.

Are you ready to go home next week?

Me: I feel ready this time, but I'm also scared I'm going to mess up. I'm scared the voice is going to tell me to restrict. I'll keep reminding myself that I deserve food. I deserve to be happy. I deserve to live.

Dr. Parker: Recovery isn't easy. It requires a lot of work and support. What you're feeling is normal. When you're struggling, you need to talk about it. Yesterday I met with Ms. Kotches, your soon-to-be high school guidance counselor. She's going to check in with you every afternoon for a while. We've put a support system in place for you. You and I will meet once per week for at least the next six months.

I feel super overwhelmed.

But I'm glad it won't be just me against the voice anymore.

Me: That sounds good.

The voice says,

(Nothing.)

Day 304

....

I say to Dr. Parker,

Thank you
for "forcing"
me to share
complicated,
hard-to-think-about thoughts.

You helped me see
anorexia nervosa
isn't really
about food.

Day 305

....

I say to Ruth,

Thank you for helping me
feel whole,
complete.

Day 310

I say to Wanda,

Thank you for helping me feed
my brain,
my heart,
my soul.

Thank you for caring about my bones.

Day 312

I say to Pedro,

Thank you for helping me express
my feelings,
my thoughts,
my heart
through art.

Day 313

Today's
my last day
inpatient at
Whispering Pines.

I've written down
and spoken
my thoughts,
my feelings,
my fears.

I've admitted
painful truths.

I've shared
how
being
bullied
feels.
I've written down

memory
after
memory,
slowly
digging
my way
out of a
deep,
dark
hole.

Light,
I see you;
I can
feel
your
warmth.

Goodbye
to the Pines
Part 1

....

Mom and I pack up my things in room
165.

Mom says,

*Dr. Parker wants to chat with you before
you're discharged.*

She'll meet you at the nurses' station.

I'll bring your things to the car.

I say,

OK! I'll see you soon.

She leaves.

I look around
room 165.

I take it all in
one last time.

I say,

I hope I never see you again,
room 165!

Goodbye
to the Pines
Part 2

As Dr. Parker and I walk through
the maze of hallways
that lead to the lobby,
she says,

*I think music, art, and theater help you
   heal.*

Stories help you make sense of the world.

*They help you tell your own story. The story
   of Jake.*

A tear
falls

d
o
w
n

my face.

I hope
I can keep
silencing
the
voice.

I think about
Grandma,
Mom,
Dad,
Ms. Burns,
Frieden,
Kella,
Ruth,
Bruce,
Pedro,
and even Izzy.
Dr. Parker says,

Jake, you have the heart of a poet.

*You can use it to do a lot of good in this
world.*

Please take care of you.

I smile as
the automatic door
S W O O S H E S
        open.

Mom's waiting for me on the other side.

I walk through.

Dr. Parker waves
as the door
closes
behind
me.

531

Skating
Reprise

....

I'm allowed to
exercise again.

Dr. Parker says,

Everything in moderation, Jake!

Moderation is key.

It's OK now
because
I know better
who I am.

And
I understand

who I am
is OK.

I dust off
my Rollerblades.

I put on my
Oak Forest High School Drama Club
T-shirt.

I insert
the *Hello, Dolly!* soundtrack
into my CD player.

I hear
Barbra Streisand's
voice.

My blood starts
pumping.

As I skate down Grandma's driveway,
I think about what Kella said yesterday
as we ate soft pretzels and drank lemonade
at Auntie Anne's in the Orland Square
  Mall:

Jake, moving into your grandma's house
with your parents and starting over in
a different school district was the new
beginning you needed.

She's right.

I love that
what used to be
my weekend bedroom
is now my everyday bedroom.

I love that it feels like Grandma will
always be close to us in this way.

I make a loop
around Pondview Park,
stopping for a moment
to say hello to
Frieden and
her four cherubs.

I think about Dr. Parker's question,
Jake, how are you feeling?
as I stand at

Frieden's base,
admiring
her pose,
feeling,
absorbing
soft light
pouring forth
from her heart.

She
gave
me
strength.

She
helped
me
feel
safe,
secure.

I look
in her
kind,

all-knowing
eyes.

I swear
she winks,
nods,
reassures me
that it's OK to take up space,
that I deserve to live.

I say,

Frieden,
I'm talking back to
the voice now.

Frieden,
I'm louder than
the voice now.

Frieden,
I'm glad you believed in me.

I wave goodbye to Frieden and her cherubs.

I wave at the
ducks.

I
sing out
at
the
top
of
my
voice.

I throw back
my head
and

SPIN

and

SPIN

and

SPIN!

....

Dear Reader,

Hello!

How are you feeling?

Thank you for reading Jake's story. Thank you for spending time with him.

His actions and reactions can make us feel uncomfortable at times.

Parts of his story are hard to read.

He's intense.

He's often confused and lost.

He often feels as though nobody will ever understand him, including himself.

For many years, he doesn't think he'll ever get better. It feels impossible.

He almost gives up a few times. But he doesn't.

He keeps moving forward, even when it hurts.

Even when he storms out of rooms and shuts down emotionally.

You might wonder what happens next in Jake's story.

I imagine . . .

1. He finds a group of accepting friends who embrace him.

2. He regularly sees a therapist who helps him express his feelings, shares tips and strategies to talk back to the voice, gives him a safe space to work through his worries, and helps him live a life that's easier, better, and more fun.

3. He asks for help when he needs it.

4. He becomes a teacher and then a school librarian.

5. He sees A LOT of Broadway shows.

6. He's loved and loves.

How do I know what Jake might do with his life?

How do I understand Jake's inner thinking?

How do I understand Jake's heart so well, so deeply?

The reality is that many of his thoughts, including his disordered thinking and eating, are based on my own experiences as a young person. His life parallels my own life in many ways. I've felt every emotion Jake experiences in the story. Many of the struggles and the situations he finds himself in are based on my own struggles and memories, but our stories aren't exactly the same. I made up characters and situations and adjusted the timeline. I fictionalized parts of my life.

I spent more than two years in and out of multiple inpatient and outpatient treatment programs and facilities for anorexia nervosa, obsessive-compulsive disorder, anxiety, and depression. I struggled day after day. I felt unworthy of taking up space. I hated myself for many years. I was stuck.

Thanks to therapy, thanks to people who cared about me, thanks to books, thanks to lots and lots of hard work, I talked back to the voice inside my head. I learned to be loud, just like Jake.

If Jake were in treatment today instead of in the 1990s, his road to

542

healing might look different. Treatment of mental and physical health evolves as clinicians learn about how our brains and bodies work, and as therapists come to new understandings about how to help different patients thrive. For many, that might include visits from family and other caregivers more regularly than what Jake experiences. Like me, Jake was often alone, because letting people in was hard. If I could talk to Jake today, I'd tell him what fourteen-year-old John didn't realize yet: that he doesn't have to do it alone! Additionally, treatment programs are now shorter than what Jake experiences. They are made up of inpatient care at facilities like Whispering Pines and then outpatient care that encourages patients to heal in their own schools or learning environments. I chose to write about Jake's journey within Whispering Pines. This allowed me to focus on the growth within him, instead of his movement between locations. Healing unfolds differently for everyone. Many factors go into the decisions that inform a treatment plan. The goal remains: health and recovery.

And recovery requires work. Every so often, the Voice wakes up. What do I do? I roar back. I reach for all the skills and strategies therapists and group therapy have taught me. I examine what's happening in my life. I identify why I'm restricting food. I ask why I'm punishing myself. I make adjustments and remember how I never want to relapse again. I remember how much better being healthy feels.

Writing Jake's story hurt and healed my heart. In other words, it was therapeutic. I took long walks as I figured out how to tell his story. I rewatched movies that comforted me as a child. I listened to the same music Jake writes about and thinks about. The movies and music helped me better understand and connect with my thirteen-year-old self.

I wanted to hug and comfort Jake many times along the way. I wanted to say, "Jake, you're going to be OK. I'll protect you. Follow your meal plan. Listen to Dr. Parker. You're worthy. You have a big, kind heart."

Thankfully, he knows how much I care about him.

If you have a big, kind heart, too, and you or someone you know may be struggling with disordered eating, please seek help. If you don't know how to ask for help, the resources and information on page 547 will give you a way to begin.

And no matter who you are, Reader, please take care of yourself! Take care of your heart!

Skate!
Sing!
Dance!
Read!
Write!
Eat!

Do what brings you joy!

Happy reading!

— John

Resources

....

Anxiety and Depression Association of
America
https://adaa.org

International OCD Foundation
https://kids.iocdf.org

National Alliance for Eating Disorders
www.allianceforeatingdisorders.com

National Association of Anorexia Nervosa
and Associated Disorders (ANAD)
https://anad.org

A Work in Progress by Jarrett Lerner
(New York: Aladdin, 2023)

*You Are Enough: Your Guide to Body Image
and Eating Disorder Recovery*
by Jen Petro-Roy
(New York: Feiwel and Friends, 2019)

Acknowledgments

....

Writing this story of my heart was a journey.

A journey of self-discovery.

A journey of bravery and vulnerability.

A journey that, as my brilliant agent, Molly O'Neill, said to me one day in New York City, expanded my heart in beautiful ways.

Yes, my heart expanded in many beautiful ways because of everyone who believed in me, challenged me, and helped me tell this story as best I could.

Molly O'Neill, you were the best advocate my heart could have hoped for as I wrote about the pain of my past. You bring so much joy and light into my life.

Susan Van Metre, your thoughtful comments showed me how much you care about Jake. With patience and understanding, you helped me dig deeper. You're an extraordinary editor and a fairy godmother.

Karen Lotz, Non Pratt, Lindsay Warren, Tracy Miracle, Sawako Shirota, Jennifer Roberts, Nancy Brennan, Julia Gaviria, Jason Emmanuel, and Emily Quill, my heart expanded because of you and everyone at Candlewick Press and Walker Books.

Maria T. Middleton and Grady McFerrin, your cover design and cover art are eye-catching and heart-expanding. Thank you!

My heart expands whenever I visit New York City. I'm grateful for every moment I spent writing and revising in the Marriott Marquis, beside the Bethesda Fountain, and during intermissions at musicals on Broadway.

My heart expanded because of friends and family who checked in with me and listened to me as I talked about the highs and lows of writing this story. I'm grateful for Paul Mullen, Lou Grant, Jasmine Warga, Donna Kouri, Margie Myers-Culver, Kate DiCamillo, Kella Hunt, Tracy van Straaten, Katherine Applegate, Lauren Castillo, Lisa Fipps, Deborah Freedman, Erin Entrada Kelly, Terry Thompson, Kelly Gustafson, Michelle

Reyes, Jennifer LaGarde, Donalyn Miller, Travis Jonker, Colby Sharp, Elly Swartz, Amy Arbizzani, Lea Anne Borders, Anne Wissinger, Dawn Molignano, the International School of Amsterdam, and every author, bookseller, educator, and librarian who has shared words in support of Jake and his story.

My heart's about to expand even more because of YOU, dear Reader.

ABOUT THE AUTHOR

John Schu is the author of the acclaimed picture books *This Is a School,* illustrated by Veronica Miller Jamison, and *This Is a Story*, illustrated by Caldecott Honoree Lauren Castillo. He also wrote the adult study *The Gift of Story: Exploring the Affective Side of the Reading Life* and was named a *Library Journal* Mover and Shaker for his dynamic interactions with students and his passionate adoption of new technologies as a means of connecting authors, illustrators, books, and readers. Children's librarian for Bookelicious, part-time lecturer at Rutgers University, and former Ambassador of School Libraries for Scholastic Book Fairs, Mr. Schu — as he is affectionately known — continues to travel the world to share his love of books. He lives in Naperville, Illinois. You can find him at www.JohnSchu.com and on social media @MrSchuReads.